JACK THE SHIFTER

BETTINA WOLFE

Jack The Shifter

ISBN-13: 9780692076170

Cover by Ana Grigoriu, Books Design

Cover photo by Emily Ives

For my father, I carry your song in my heart, always.

One more game and then I'm done.

The glow from the computer lit up her face. She was logged into game room seven on the Flash Star Poker website, under the screen name SaraGirl25. Jack of Spades was there again, seated in the spot right next to her. He had been there every night for the past two weeks, watching her.

They were playing their usual game, Texas hold 'em. When the fifth and final card was dealt face up on the table, she considered three options: fold, check or bet.

Without hesitation, she clicked on 'bet.' Moments later, the word 'winner' blazed above her screen name, she had hit a straight flush.

A message soon appeared in the chat box area below.

Jack_of_ Spades: Great hand, SaraGirl.

Pausing for a moment, she typed a reply.

SaraGirl25: Thanks, I'm still learning how to play.

Jack_of_Spades: Not too bad for a beginner. I have seen you here a few times before.

SaraGirl25: Yeah, your screen name looks familiar too.

Jack_of_Spades: You know what they say, 'Practice makes perfect.'

SaraGirl25: I guess. Anyhow, it's late. I was about to log off.

Jack_of_Spades: Well then, SaraGirl, good night and good luck.

"Good night Jack of Spades," she whispered to the screen.

Weary-eyed, Sara leaned back in her chair. Stretching her arms toward the ceiling, she clasped her hands and rested them behind her neck. *Playing games is not going to pay the bills.*

Sara had been out of work for five months. She was laid off from her executive assistant position at Clearmont Telecom. Due to a merger, the company had axed more than eight hundred jobs. Her boss, Stewart Gritley, VP of Operations, was also let go. It thrilled her because she loathed the little troll (the secret pet name she had given him).

Stewart, a short pudgy man, sported a greasy comb-over on top of his head. His collection of ill-fitting, wrinkled dress shirts looked as if he'd slept in them. He stood no more than five feet-five inches tall. Sara, at five-seven, towered over him in her four-inch pumps that she wore every day. It annoyed him to no end to look up to anyone, let alone Sara.

Stewart's daily temper tantrums would send papers flying into the air and fluttering to the floor. She would always rush to clean up after his childish outbursts. His voice was raucous and he talked too much, constantly yapping and whining like an anxious little Chihuahua.

Sara's blood would boil when the first thing, each morning, he would park himself at her cubicle. Leaning over her desk, he would juggle a cappuccino in one hand and a powdered doughnut in the other. Between bites, as he rattled off her daily to-do list, sprinkles of fine sugar would fall, dusting her notepad as she tried to write. He would lap at his cappuccino, slurping it, and chomp on his doughnut with his mouth open.

While Sara was ecstatic to be rid of Stewart, she was unhappy about losing her job. Despite the hostile work environment, the money was good, and she was grateful for the two-month severance package she had received. Sara, however, had never planned for a rainy day. At twenty-nine years of age, she didn't have a dime in savings.

A few months before she lost her job, she had redecorated her modest one-bedroom apartment, maxing out all of her credit cards. Although her new white tufted headboard was pleasing to look at, it didn't comfort her at night as she lay restless. She needed to find a job. Fast.

During the day Sara spent hours online, scouring the classifieds and sending out résumés. When evening arrived, she would log into the gaming sites to play cards. It had all started last month as a way of relieving stress and helping to clear her head.

Heck, maybe I should play with real money, try to make a living out of it, she caught herself thinking. But then a little voice in the back of her head spoke, *Okay Sara, enough. So you won a few fake money games. You're not 'that' good of a player. You need to get some sleep.*

Sara yawned, her eyelids feeling heavy. Closing her laptop, she stood up from the small corner desk in her bedroom and crawled into bed.

Jack of Spades watched SaraGirl25 log off. He was the only one left in the game room. He waited for another player, another chance to connect with someone.

Slouched behind his cluttered desk, he sat in silence. An icy draft circled the room, and a dusty lamp light flickered beside him. The big old house on the lake felt empty again.

On the wall, an antique cuckoo clock chimed twelve times.

Midnight.

After pushing himself out of the tattered leather chair, he shuffled toward the large picture window in the living room.

Staring out into the vast darkness, he stood motionless. The night sky, illuminated with stars, reflected in the lake below. The water remained still, a sheet of speckled black glass. There was no wind, no movement. All was quiet. An eerie dead calm.

2

The next morning, Sara awoke exhausted. A dull ache stretched across her brow. Her ears rang inside her head; a piercing high-pitched sound. She had tossed and turned all night. The strain of unemployment was disquieting, affecting her quality of sleep.

Dragging herself out of bed, she reached for the white terrycloth robe hanging on the back of the door. She slipped into the robe and tied the belt tight around her waist. With half-closed eyes, she padded her way to the kitchen and reached for the glass jar of coffee beans on the countertop.

This is the way she started her day, every day. Her days had become routine. Wake up, brew coffee, job search, eat lunch, job search, take shower, eat dinner, play games, go to sleep. Awake and repeat.

As the early morning sun shone brightly through the small

kitchen window, she leaned back against the counter. Closing her eyes, she dozed off as the sun warmed her face.

A few minutes later, three faint beeps sounded in the distance, signaling her that the coffee had finishing brewing. She poured the steaming coffee into a mug, stirred in two spoons of sugar and a splash of vanilla soy milk. With both hands wrapped around the mug, she inhaled the sweet aroma and made her way back to the bedroom.

Setting the mug on her desk, she flipped open her computer and plopped down in her chair. She stared at the screen as it powered up, dreading another day of job hunting.

After taking a sip of coffee, she did something she'd never done in the morning or the daytime. It was something she only allowed herself to do in the evenings and late at night.

She logged into the Flash Star Poker website.

I'll just play one quick game before checking the job boards.

Scrolling through the page, she paused, the blinking cursor hovering over game room seven. With the click of the mouse, she entered the game. Scanning the player's avatars, she saw him, Jack of Spades, in seat number three. Seconds later, a message from him popped up in the chat box.

Jack_of_Spades: Good Morning, SaraGirl. What brings you here so early today?

SaraGirl25: Good Morning, I was about to ask you the same question.

Jack_of_Spades: I am simply here honing my craft. And you are doing what?

SaraGirl25: I can't seem to focus this morning.

Jack_of_Spades: Are you okay?

SaraGirl25: I'm just tired and stressed.

Jack_of_Spades: Why are you stressed?

SaraGirl25: I've been out of work for a few months.

Jack_of_Spades: Sorry to hear that, Sara, if Sara is your real name.

SaraGirl25: Yes, it's my name, Sara Tyler.

Confused by the words staring back at her on the screen, a lump formed in her throat. *Why did I tell him my name?* She sighed. She took another sip of coffee.

Jack_of_Spades: Pleased to meet you, Miss Tyler. My name is Jack Halvrek.

SaraGirl25: Nice to meet you, Jack. Now, if you'll excuse me, I need to get back to my job search.

Jack_of_Spades: Sara, just a minute, please. Before you go, may I ask what type of work you do?

SaraGirl25: I am, I mean, was, an executive assistant but I was laid off.

Jack_of_Spades: Oh, you lost your job, I see. Where do you live?

SaraGirl25: I don't give out my address online. I need to go.

Jack_of_Spades: Of course, I understand. Well, listen. I am looking for someone to assist me with a poker tournament I am hosting, here at my estate.

SaraGirl25: A tournament?

Jack_of_Spades: Yes. You know, Sara, it is difficult to find good help these days.

SaraGirl25: I can relate. It's getting tougher out there to find a decent job.

Jack_of_Spades: Well then, I will not keep you. You sound like a respectable young lady who now finds herself in a bit of a bind. I thought we might have been able to help each other. I thought perhaps you could assist me with things, help me organize the tournament. I was also hoping you lived somewhere nearby. I reside in Grand County, Colorado.

While hesitant to reply, Sara sensed desperation in his words. *Maybe he genuinely needs help.*

Jack_of_Spades: Are you still there? Did I lose you? I apologize. Perhaps this attempt was all a shot in the dark.

SaraGirl25: I'm still here. I live in Denver.

Jack_of_Spades: Denver? You are only two hours away. Perhaps we could meet in person to discuss the tournament, and then you can decide if you would like to help me with it. I am thinking somewhere halfway. What about Cliffstown?

SaraGirl25: Cliffstown? I'm about an hour from there.

Jack_of_Spades: Well then, would you like to meet for coffee in the morning, say around ten? We can meet at Café Remillard on Main Street.

Pressing her lips together, she stared at the screen, weighing the risks. *A public place … daytime … it should be safe.*

SaraGirl25: Okay, I guess I could meet you there.

Jack_of_Spades: Wonderful. I look forward to meeting you. Oh, Sara, how will I know it is you? Please tell me a little something, perhaps the color of your hair.

She felt a slight twinge in her stomach but ignored it.

SaraGirl25: Strawberry blonde.

Jack_of_Spades: Very well then. I will be waiting for you, seated at a table in the back of the café. You will see a man with salt and pepper hair. He will be wearing a black and red western style shirt, blue jeans, and cowboy boots.

Sara reread his words. *That's a little strange. Why does it sound like he's describing someone else?*

As she placed her fingers back on the keyboard, she glanced above the chat box area. They were the only two players seated at the table. Everyone else had left the room.

SaraGirl25: Okay, Jack, I'll see you tomorrow.

Jack_of_Spades: Until then, Sara.

Sara logged out of the game room and opened a new tab in her browser, searching for the name Jack Halvrek.

She scrolled and clicked through the first few pages but found nothing. *There has to be something posted somewhere about him.* Next page, *click.* And there it was.

On page five, his name appeared a few times. She read all the entries. After viewing each one, the only information she could find were contributions to various charitable organizations. He'd made many considerable donations over the years, thousands of dollars.

Maybe there's no reason to worry.

3

Sara stood in front of her new full-length floor mirror, tugging at the sleeves of her cardigan and adjusting her black pencil skirt. Her clothes were fitting a little too tight. She was uncomfortable and breaking out in a sweat. She had gained a few pounds over the past few months binging on comfort food. Macaroni and cheese plus potato chips, two of her all time favorites.

Lifting her hair off her shoulders, she fanned the back of her neck with her hand. She wasn't sure if she was sweating from having changed clothes three times, or from not knowing whether she had made the right decision to meet a random online stranger. What she did know, though, was that she was running late. Her watch read 9:05 a.m.

With Friday traffic, it was at least an hour drive to

Cliffstown. *This outfit will have to do.* Grabbing her keys and black tote bag, she rushed out the front door.

Outside the air was unusually warm for late October. The sun shone bright, wispy, white clouds lingered above. A gentle breeze cooled her heated skin as she dashed down the concrete steps of her second-floor apartment.

With her keys jingling, she scurried toward the carport. Clicking the key fob, the doors unlocked, and she climbed inside, fastening her seat belt. She searched through her tote bag and pulled out her iPhone.

Pressing and holding down the lower button, she spoke, "Directions."

"Where would you like to go?" The partly human, partly robotic voice asked.

"Café Remillard."

"Getting directions to Café Remillard."

Placing her phone in the cup holder, she turned the key in the ignition and started the engine.

Traffic was moderate on the I-70 west freeway. In her blue Audi A4, Sara sped along, weaving in and out of the lanes, panicky and perspiring.

She turned on the air conditioner and adjusted the vent, aiming it directly at her face. Despite pushing the button to the coldest setting, it continued to blow hot air. Flustered, she put the windows down, the wind whipping her hair across her face. She worried that either the air conditioning unit or something else might need to be replaced. She had heard unfamiliar sounds coming from the engine lately.

No extra money was available for car repairs, not after her redecorating spree. Even though the loan on her car was paid off, every so often her little dream car gently reminded her, everything comes with a price.

"In five hundred feet, the destination will be on your right."

She gazed ahead.

"Arrived."

Sara slowed the car to a crawl. She felt as if she had traveled back in time to a Victorian village. Quaint, colorful structures dotted the main street, housing small shops and restaurants. The buildings, fully restored from the 1800s, were reminiscent of an era gone by.

Spotting a small parking area to her left, she accelerated, entering the lot and parking the car. It was just after ten o'clock. While angling the rear-view mirror, she quickly ran a brush through her hair. Slinging her tote bag over her shoulder, she exited the car and hurried to the front of the café.

When she reached out to grip the iron door handle, a rusted horseshoe hanging above the entrance caught her eye. *Maybe it's my lucky day.* The barn wood door creaked on its hinges as she pulled it open.

Inside the café, black and white cowboy photos and Western memorabilia graced the walls. The smell of sizzling bacon and sweet maple syrup wafted in the air.

Glancing around at the handful of diners, Sara heard music playing softly in the background. After scanning the bar stools and a few booths by the window, she remembered the words Jack had told her. *I will be waiting for you, seated at a table in the back of the café.*

She focused her eyes on the back corner tables. *You will see a man with salt and pepper hair.* Walking through the café, she saw an older man, seated at a table near the exit door. Dressed in a black and red western shirt and jeans, he was reading the menu.

The closer she moved toward him, the louder her heels clicked against the hardwood floor. Lifting his head, the man gazed at her as she walked up to the table. Grinning ear to ear, he sprang from his chair and extended his hand.

"Sara? Is it you?" he asked.

"Jack? Hi, I'm Sara." With a timid smile, she shook his hand.

"It is a pleasure to meet you, Miss Tyler. Please join me, have a seat." His fingers brushed her shoulder as he motioned for her to sit.

Sara pulled out the small wooden chair and sat across from him, placing her tote bag on the chair beside her. Jack narrowed his eyes, his smile fading.

"You are late," he quipped.

"I'm sorry. I hit some traffic on my way here." Sweat beaded on her face.

"Do you know the rules of the game?" His bushy eyebrows danced like two fuzzy caterpillars.

"Never let them see you sweat?" Wiping her forehead with the back of her hand, she reached for the glass of water sitting on the table.

His eyes softened, the grin reappearing on his sun-weathered face. "Well, one rule, a rather important one, states: know thy opponent."

"Opponent?" she asked, tipping her head to the side.

"Yes, I must know with whom I am dealing. There are others who have offered to help me. You are not the only one."

"Oh, of course. You need my references." Reaching into her tote bag, she pulled out a thin black portfolio and handed him her résumé, her hands trembling.

"Are you nervous?"

"No, sometimes I become a little lightheaded. I have low blood sugar."

Jack gestured for the waiter while she peeked at the menu. He gave her résumé a cursory glance and set it aside.

"Sara, although this piece of paper informs me of your qualifications and experience, it does not tell me about you," he said, his gaze intensifying.

The waiter, a lanky young man, approached the table.

Before he could introduce himself, Jack looked him in the eye and barked out an order.

"I will have a cup of coffee with extra cream, blueberry pancakes, and a side of bacon."

The waiter jotted down the items on a small notepad and glanced over at Sara. "And what can I get for you, miss?" he asked, tapping his pen on the pad.

Glimpsing at the name tag pinned to the waiter's shirt, she offered a friendly smile.

"Hello, Ryan. May I have a glass of orange juice?"

"Is that all?" he asked.

"On second thought, I'll also have a bowl of oatmeal, please." Reaching for both menus, she handed them to Ryan. He smiled, thanked her, and walked away.

Jack was fixated on Sara, studying her features. Her strawberry blonde hair fell in long layers, framing her face. Thick lashes fringed her jade green eyes, and a smattering of freckles dotted her nose and cheeks. Her lips had been glossed with a shade of petal pink.

"So please, tell me about yourself," he urged, his eyebrows dancing again.

Ryan returned with their beverages. Sara grasped the glass of orange juice and drank half, guzzling it, and then cleared her throat.

"I'm detail oriented and work well under pressure. I can type seventy-five words a minute. I have excellent time-management skills, great organizational skills and I—"

"Sara, please," he held up his hand, "that is all well and good. Now, when can you start helping me?" his gaze deepened.

"Start?" She looked away and then back at him. "I don't even know what you need help with."

"Well, I have already told you I need help with the tournament. It is quite simple. I need help with organizing things at my estate. There is much work to do to prepare for the event, and I was hoping to find someone to assist me." His leathered face softened, losing all expression. Shrugging his shoulders, he slouched in the chair.

A rush of sadness fell over Sara. She sensed an underlying despair in his voice.

"You don't have anyone to help you?" she asked, tilting her head to the side. "Any family...or friends?"

He let out a breath, placing his hand on his chest. "You see, during the last tournament, I almost had a heart attack."

"Heart attack?" her voice cracked.

"Yes, unfortunately, there was a little, shall I say, incident." Leaning on the table, he looked her straight in the eye. "That is why I need someone to assist me." His lips quivered to a smirk.

Tears welled in her eyes.

"Sara, what is wrong? Was it something I said that upset you?"

She knew it wasn't the time or place to talk about her personal life, but her emotions, as always, got the best of her. "My dad…my father…he died of a heart attack last year."

"I am sorry to hear that." Reaching into his back pocket, he withdrew his handkerchief and offered it to her.

Moments later, Ryan returned with their breakfast. After placing the dishes on the table, he glanced at them and took a step back.

"May I get either of you anything else?"

"No, that will be all. Bring the check in fifteen minutes." Jack lifted his hand, shooing him away.

"Sara, I did not mean to recall the memory of your father and make you cry."

"It's okay, I'm all right." Sniffling, she dabbed the tears from her eyes.

"It is difficult to lose," he said. "I lost my mother when I was young, younger than you. She died in a riding accident. I saw it happen, right in front of me. Remember it as if it were yesterday. It was a Saturday, late September, one of the darkest days of my life."

"Oh Jack, I'm so sorry." Her tears returned. "I can't even imagine."

"Yes, well, that is all in the past. Nothing we can do about it today. We must keep them safe in our memories. Life does go on."

Their conversation fell silent as the background music grew louder. Jack shoveled down his syrup-soaked pancakes, while Sara took tiny spoonfuls of her oatmeal. Jack began waving his fork side to side as if he were conducting an orchestra.

The café was playing a golden oldie, the tune somewhat familiar. Sara straightened her posture and leaned her ear toward the small speaker above the table.

Doris Day's contralto voice flowed over the table as she sang her signature song, "Que sera, sera, whatever will be, will be."

Jack focused his eyes on her and started singing his own version of the song in an unsteady, baritone voice.

"Say Sara, Sara. What will your answer be? Will you say yes to me? Say Sara, Sara."

Half smiling, she squirmed in her seat.

Ryan soon reappeared at the table. Apparently he thought Jack was beckoning him with the fork. "Would either of you like more coffee?" he asked, reaching out to remove their plates.

"No, but I would like you to tell this pretty young lady to say yes to my offer." Jack shifted his gaze, pointing at Sara. Ryan shot him a quick half smile, placed the bill on the table and walked away.

"Sara, now returning to my offer, I will need your assistance for a week. It should be enough time for me to restore order in my house and prepare for the tournament. After the last event, things have, well, fallen by the wayside, so to speak. Therefore, I will need you to start tomorrow."

"Tomorrow?" she repeated in disbelief.

"Yes, the tournament is next weekend. Now let us move on to the details. Six players will be arriving to participate in a game called Jack the Shifter."

"Jack the Shifter? I've never heard of it."

"It is a variant of seven card stud. When a player is dealt a face-up Jack, the game changes."

"Changes?"

"Yes," he leaned in toward her, "a Jack will always change the game." Arching his eyebrows, he grinned.

"Change the game to what?"

"Well, there is a bit more to it," he said, waggling his fingers. "We will go over all the rules when everyone arrives. However, it is important to know that each player will enter the game with a three thousand dollar buy-in."

"Buy-in?"

"Yes, it is the entry fee. However, if you help me organize, I will give you the buy-in for assisting me. You can either keep the three thousand dollars or use it to enter the game. If you decide to participate, you will be player number seven. With seven players, the prize pool will be twenty-one thousand dollars."

Sara blinked rapidly.

"I have watched you play for some time, and I believe your chance of winning is quite high. I would think twenty-one thousand dollars would help a young lady in your situation, would it not?" Leaning back in his chair, he anticipated her reply.

Three thousand for a week, and the chance to win twenty-one thousand dollars.

"What do you say, Sara? Are you interested?" He drummed his fingers on the table.

"It's a gracious offer, thank you. But it would be a long commute, back and forth. If I'm not mistaken, Grand County is a two-hour drive from the city."

"Perhaps I forgot to mention, you will stay with me." A sheepish grin formed on his face.

"Stay with you?" her voice squeaked. A knot twisted in her stomach.

"Why, of course. I would not expect you to drive so far each day. You will have your own room, and you will have four rooms from which to choose."

Sara remained polite. "Jack, I appreciate your offer. But to be honest, I'm not sure I'd be comfortable staying in your house. I've only just met you and I don't know much about your background."

"Well, what exactly would you like to know?" Raising his eyebrows, he crossed his arms in front of his chest and glared at her.

"I'll need to think it over a bit...to make an appropriate decision."

Flicking his wrist, he checked his watch and huffed. "Sara, we have run out of time here. I must leave for my next appointment."

Picking up her résumé, he folded it in perfect quarters and tucked it into the front pocket of his shirt. He shot up from the chair and reached for his wallet chained to his belt. He pulled out a twenty and a ten and tossed them on the table to cover the bill.

His boots thudded across the floor as he walked away. Stopping for a moment, he half turned and glanced back at her.

"Think it over, Sara. Take the risk or lose the chance," he said, his voice echoing through the café as he headed toward the door.

Sara rose from her chair to use the restroom. When she exited the lavatory, Ryan was cleaning the table. She strolled over to him.

"Ryan, excuse me, can I ask you something?"

"Yeah, sure. What's up?"

"The man I was with. Have you seen him here before?"

"The one with the freaky eyes? Nope. I'd remember a guy like that."

"Like what?" she asked, riffling through her tote bag for her keys.

"Not sure, but I kinda got a weird vibe from him."

"Hmm, okay." She let out a tiny giggle. "Thanks, Ryan, have a nice day."

With keys in hand, Sara walked through the café. She had a funny feeling Jack might be out front waiting for her. As she stepped outside, she squinted against the sun's glare. A few pedestrians bustled along the sidewalk. She looked to the left, and then to the right. There was no sign of him.

Crossing the street, she entered the parking lot. She surveyed the cars, examining each one with care. When she was certain he was gone, she slipped into her car and drove away.

4

Zooming down the highway, on her way home, Sara replayed the breakfast meeting in her head. *Three thousand to help him organize and a chance at winning twenty-one thousand dollars. But there's a catch…he wants me to stay at his house.*

As she approached the exit, she signaled with her blinker. The service engine light flashed on the dashboard. Her car was due for routine maintenance, the odometer reading just over ninety-nine thousand miles.

After exiting the off-ramp, she figured she would swing by the auto dealership. She would pass by it anyhow, as Foxdale Audi was located a few blocks from her apartment.

She entered the lot and pulled up alongside the giant white building. Staring into the large glass showroom windows, she reflected on the day she had purchased her sporty little sedan.

Although it was a used car, it was new to Sara. But it was a car she'd never planned on buying.

One day, years ago, a co-worker dragged her to Foxdale on their lunch hour. Allison, who was also Sara's friend, had her eye on an Audi A4. It was all she ever talked about.

At the time, Sara was more than content with her old beat-up Jeep Wrangler until that day during their lunch hour... during an unforgettable test drive.

When Allison sat behind the wheel of the car, the salesman took his place in the passenger seat and Sara relaxed in the back. Allison exited the dealership, drove down a few side streets, and proceeded in the direction of the highway. The second she reached the end of the on-ramp, the slick salesman encouraged her to drive faster.

"C'mon, girl, let's see what this car can do," he shouted.

"Yeah, step on it," Sara chimed in. "This car is meant to be driven. Do you want me to show you how it's done?"

Despite both the salesman and Sara cheering Allison on, she barely hit 55 miles per hour on the highway.

Upon returning to the car lot, the salesman guided her to a wide open area out back. Wanting to show her the way the car handled on turns, he urged her to do a donut. While Allison attempted to do the circular maneuver, she tensed up, panicking behind the wheel. The only squealing that day came from Allison's lungs, not the tires.

At the end of the test drive, when Sara climbed out of the car, the salesman slipped her his business card. "Come back and see me sometime and we'll go for a spin," he said. She smiled cautiously at him. Beneath her demure demeanor, she was a pedal-to-the-metal type of gal. The salesman must have sensed that one day she would return.

Giving her thoughts a mental shake, Sara proceeded around the building to the service area. A tall, attractive, dark-haired man wearing a navy work shirt and cargo pants walked over to greet her. Wiping his hand along the side of his pants, he reached out and opened the driver's side door.

"Good afternoon, I'm Kenny. Do you have an appointment?"

"No, sorry, I don't," she fretted. "My check-engine light is on."

"No worries, we're not too busy today. I'm sure we can squeeze you in and take a look." Flashing her a perfect white smile, he looked to be around the same age as Sara.

Gathering her tote bag, Sara stepped out of her car and smoothed her skirt. Kenny invited her to wait inside and then drove her car to the rear of the building. She swung open the large glass door and wandered over to a seat by the window.

While waiting for her car, she mulled over Jack's offer. *He seemed a little eccentric...but it's only for a week. Could I really win twenty-one thousand dollars? I guess I have as good a chance as anyone else.*

Sara gazed up and saw a lady helping a frail, white-haired woman settle into a chair across from her. They appeared to be mother and daughter. As Sara caught hold of the senior woman's eye, she smiled at her. The woman slightly raised a shaky hand and waved hello. At that moment Sara remembered she had forgotten to call her mom.

Every other day, at nine in the morning, Sara would call her mother. Helen Tyler lived in an assisted living community. Soon after Sara's father died, her mom's health had declined and she developed dementia. Although Helen was having trouble remembering things, she always seemed to know when Sara forgot to call and would often remind her of that oversight.

Sara pulled her cell phone out of her tote bag, swiped through the favorites on her contact list and pressed 'M.'

"Good afternoon, Sun Meadows Assisted Care, how may I help you?"

"Hello, may I please speak to Helen Tyler?"

"One moment please, I'll transfer you."

The phone rang five times.

"Hello," a weak voice rattled on the other end.

"Hi mom, it's me."

"Sara? Where are you?" Helen sounded confused.

"At the dealership having my car checked. The engine light came on when I was driving home from a meeting. I'm hoping it's nothing serious."

"Are you okay? Are you sick?"

"Yes, I'm okay and no, I'm not sick. Do you need anything?"

"I'm watching TV, my show is on," her voice escalated.

"Okay, I'll let you watch your show. Love you."

"Bye-bye." *Click.* Helen hung up.

Staring at the cell phone clenched in her hand, Sara sighed sorrowfully. Tears pooled in her eyes. It hurt to hear her mother's memory deteriorating, and each call to her mom broke Sara's heart more and more.

Growing up as an only child, Sara remembered how vivacious her mother used to be. From gardening to ceramic and dance classes, Helen had led an active lifestyle. Sara's fondest memories were the weekends they spent baking together. Helen's cookies and desserts were second to none. Her sweet confections would satisfy the most discerning chocoholic. She was always trying out new recipes, and Sara was her number one taste-tester.

At one point, Helen had talked about opening a specialty coffee shop and bakery. Sara wished her mom would have followed her dream. She was certain it would have been a great success.

Sara sat clicking through her phone when Kenny walked over to her, a piece of white paper dangling from his hand. This time he wasn't smiling.

"Sara, I have good news and bad news," he blurted.

"What's the good news?"

"The good news is we can have your car fixed in a couple of days."

"And the bad news?" She gritted her teeth.

"More than one thing needs repair. The cost, parts and labor, comes to fourteen hundred and twenty-five dollars."

"Oh no," she moaned. "What's wrong with my car?"

Kenny passed her the sheet of paper, each line followed by a dollar sign.

"Is it safe for me to drive home?"

"No, afraid not." His tone was firm. "Don't worry, we'll fix it. I'll need you to sign at the bottom that you agree to the charges."

"How can I agree to any charges when I can't afford to pay them?" Studying the paper, she frowned. She knew her next move. Taking a deep breath, she looked up at him.

"Would it be okay to keep my car here for a week or so? I'm between jobs right now and need a little time to raise the money."

"I'm sure it'll be fine. I'll let my manager know." Reaching into his pocket he handed her a business card. "Call me if you need anything," he winked.

"Okay, I appreciate your help." Sara stood up and started walking toward the door. Forgetting something, she turned around.

"Oh Kenny...I need the house keys off my key ring, please."

"No problem, give me a minute and I'll grab them for you.

If you'd like, our courtesy van can take you home." He smiled.

"That would be great, thank you."

While Sara waited for her ride, she mapped out a game plan in her head. She would accept Jack's offer but ask him for half of the buy-in money up front. She needed fourteen hundred dollars. She needed her car in working condition for the drive to Grand County.

———

Later that evening, back at her apartment, Sara was cooking dinner when her cell phone buzzed on the kitchen counter. She kept her phone close by at all times, always within reach. Glancing at the screen, it showed 'caller unknown.' She let it buzz a few more times before deciding to answer it.

"Hello."

"Hello, Sara? This is Jack."

"Oh, hi Jack, how are you?"

"Are you busy?"

"I'm making dinner," she said, as she stirred a small pot of crushed tomatoes on the stove.

"What are you cooking?"

"Spaghetti with marinara sauce."

"Ooh, my favorite, I will be there in a few."

"You don't know where I live."

"No, but I could find out." His voice sounded gruff. "Tell me, how was the rest of your day?"

A long pause ensued. She lowered the heat under the pot of boiling water.

"Not so good," she sighed.

"Oh, why is that?"

"On my way home, after our meeting this morning, I had a little car trouble. It's in the shop right now because, well…I'm embarrassed to say this, but, I can't afford to have it repaired."

"Shall I assume then, you will accept my offer?"

"Yes, as soon as I can have my car fixed. Jack…I was thinking…would it be possible for you to advance me half—"

"Sara, as I mentioned, I need you to start tomorrow. I will drive to the city and pick you up. No need to stress about your car."

"But I want my car with me. I need my car with me."

"Sara, you will have a car here to drive. I have two vehicles. Now, what is your address, please?"

She hesitated for a few seconds. "Why don't we meet halfway? I can take a taxi and meet you in Cliffstown at the café where we had breakfast."

"Okay, Sara, as you wish. See you tomorrow, twelve noon sharp." Jack ended the call.

After Sara finished her dinner, she went into the bedroom to pack. While the thought of winning thousands of dollars excited her, she felt uneasy, her stomach flip-flopping. Searching in the far end of the narrow closet, she pulled out a navy soft-sided suitcase plus a small canvas duffle bag and placed them on the bed. She rummaged through her closet, grabbing a week's worth of pants, sweaters, tee-shirts, and jeans.

Folding her clothes, she tucked them into the suitcase. She reached down for two pairs of shoes, placed them in the side pockets and zipped the suitcase.

As she raked through her dresser drawers gathering underwear and pajamas, she flung them on the bed. Her momentary excitement soon turned to irritation.

"I want to drive my car, not his," she whined out loud. Sara's car was her source of freedom, her source of control. She hated playing the role of passenger as she much preferred to be the driver.

Marching into the bathroom, she collected her toiletries from the vanity and put them in a cosmetic travel case. She tossed her remaining items in the duffle bag and sat on the edge of the bed.

Am I crazy? Am I that desperate to be packing to leave for some stranger's house?

5

At 10:45 on Saturday morning, the taxi driver beeped his horn outside Sara's apartment. She collected her bags, stepped out the front door and placed them on the landing. Fumbling with her keys, she locked the door and jiggled the handle, making sure it was firmly locked behind her.

Dressed casually, she was wearing a gray tunic top, jeans, and a pair of well-worn ballet flats. Her hair was tied back into a sleek ponytail, and aviator sunglasses balanced on her head.

The shaggy-haired driver hopped out of his yellow cab and climbed the steps to her apartment. Picking up her suitcase and duffle bag, he carried them back down the stairs. She held onto the railing as she followed behind him with her tote bag strapped over her shoulder.

Sara crawled into the back seat while the driver loaded her

luggage into the trunk. The smell of black cherry permeated the taxi, the pungency making her throat constrict. She coughed, in need of air.

As she opened the rear window, she glanced up at her apartment. Perched on the railing of the building, a black crow darted its head, cawing loudly. She kept her eyes focused on the large, glossy bird as it fluttered its wings and continued to caw.

The driver slid behind the wheel and looked back at Sara with intense, deep-set dark eyes. He nodded his head toward the railing.

"Sounds like that bird is trying to tell ya something," he said, his voice low and raspy. Eyeballing her through his rearview mirror, he waited for an answer. She gazed at him, then back at the crow. A cold shiver ran down her spine.

The drive to Cliffstown took an hour. When they pulled onto Main Street, Sara craned her neck in the direction of the café. From a distance, she saw a man standing next to a car. As the taxi neared, she could see it was Jack, leaning against a crimson Cadillac sedan. He was reading a newspaper.

"You can drop me here, please," Sara pointed to his car. Gathering her belongings, she checked her watch, 11:45 a.m. The driver pulled up to the curb and then turned his head to her. She reached into her tote for her wallet.

Jack folded the newspaper, tossed it in his car, and then waltzed over to the taxi. Poking his head in the driver's side window, he eyed the meter, seeing the fare read ninety-three dollars and twenty-six cents. He reached into the front pocket of his jeans and pulled out a wad of cash. Licking his finger, he peeled off a hundred-dollar bill and a fifty and handed them to the driver.

"Keep the change," he gloated.

Peeking into the backseat, he smiled at Sara while smacking his chewing gum. He curled his fingers around the handle and opened the back door.

"Well, good morning, Miss Tyler. It is so nice to see you again, and on time for once," he held out his wrist, pointing to his watch.

Sara scooched across the seat, stepped out of the taxi, and stood facing him. She noticed he wore the same clothes as the day before: black and red western style shirt, blue jeans, and cowboy boots.

"Good morning," she said. "I tried to beat you this time, arriving a little early today."

"My dear, try as you may to beat me but know you will never win." His steel gray eyes didn't blink.

Sara's posture stiffened. Something about his eyes disturbed her. For a moment she thought about crawling back into the taxi until she heard the trunk slam shut, jolting her back to the present. The driver placed her luggage by her side, and in an instant, he was gone.

Jack patted her on the shoulder, picked up her bags, and strode over to his Cadillac. A wary smile surfaced on her lips as she followed him. After placing her luggage in the back seat, he held open the front passenger-side door and waited until she climbed in.

As he crossed in front of his car, he eyed her through the windshield with a devilish grin. A feeling of dread washed over her. *Did I make the right decision?*

He opened his door and sank into the driver's seat. "And we are off," he said, turning toward her.

Sara buckled her seat belt and seconds later the door locks clicked. The Cadillac cruised down Main Street and turned left.

"So tell me about this car of yours. What seems to be wrong with it?" he asked.

"Oh, a few different things are costing me fourteen hundred dollars for repairs."

"I see. What kind of car do you have?"

"Audi A4, I bought it used, years ago. It's been fine until now. Anyhow, it's at the service shop…until I can pay for the repairs." She exhaled and tried not to think about her car.

As they turned onto the highway, Sara couldn't help but notice the little, tan bobble-head dog on top of the dashboard. It was nodding its head 'yes,' and shaking its head 'no.' She could relate to the dog's indecisiveness. Jack looked over and caught her staring at it.

"His name is Tommy."

"Whose name is Tommy?" she asked, confused.

"The dog. His name is Tommy."

He picked up the bobble-head toy and shook it in front of her face. "Tommy says he is pleased to meet you," he said, speaking the words in a high-pitched voice. Placing the dog back on the dashboard, he turned to her with a wide grin.

Sara bit down on her tongue for a second to hold back a laugh. She sensed she better play along. "Nice to meet you, too, Tommy," she replied, nodding back at the toy.

Jack turned the stereo on and the sounds of classical music filled the car. He kept the volume low as he hummed along to the melodies.

Sara tried to relax and enjoy the change of scenery after being cooped up in her apartment all summer. Peering out the passenger-side window, she focused on the brilliant orange and red leaves covering the trees. Although spring was her favorite time of year, autumn was second. Spring was full of hope and new beginnings; autumn brought transition and awareness. With slight apprehension, she was looking forward to the change of pace.

While resting her head against the cool leather seat, she gazed out the window. The further north they drove, the taller the pine trees grew. The road became narrow, winding through the mountain, and they soon reached an elevation of ten thousand feet. With both hands on the steering wheel, Jack tapped his thumbs along to the music.

Sara caught a glimpse of a road sign as it whizzed past her

window, yellow with a black squiggly arrow. Looking ahead, her eyes opened wide. The road curved to the right, then twisted to the left. All she could see was the steep, rock drop-off to her right. No guard rails buffered them. Panicking, her palms grew clammy and her pulse raced.

Out of nowhere, a squirrel scampered across the road and the car ahead of them abruptly stopped. Jack swerved, slamming on the brakes. The Cadillac skidded, its wheels screeching before coming to a halt on the side of the road. Sara heard a thunk and looked over at Jack.

A handgun had slid out from under his seat. He reached down by his foot, picked up his revolver, and quickly shoved it back under the seat. Staring at him, she froze like a deer in the headlights. She could feel the blood draining from her face.

"What is it? Have you never seen a gun before?" he asked, unnaturally calm, glancing at her then to his rearview mirror.

"N-n-not unexpectedly," she stuttered, her whole body trembling.

Turning the wheel, Jack eased the car back onto the roadway.

"Well, my dear, there is no need to panic. This old cowboy has been carrying since the day he could walk. I carry it for protection only. Sit back and relax, we have an hour until we reach our destination."

Relax? Are you kidding me? We almost went careening

over a cliff. A gun? Old cowboy? What the hell is going on here?

Wiping her wet palms on her jeans, she took five deep breaths, willing her heart rate to slow, begging her stomach to stop churning.

"Sara, let me ask you something. What is it that you fear?"

"Oh," catching her breath, "a few different things, such as a fear of heights for one."

"Ah yes, acrophobia."

"What about you?" Swallowing hard, she took another breath. "What do you fear?"

"Not much," he replied. "Well, wait," he turned to look at her, "perhaps there is one thing I fear."

"One thing?"

"Yes, one thing. Autophobia."

"Autophobia?" She paused for a moment, squinting her eyes. "You're afraid of cars? That makes no sense."

"No, that is not what it is," shaking his head.

"Well, then what does it mean?"

"You are a smart girl. You will figure it out."

Gripping the steering wheel, Jack kept his gaze locked on the road ahead.

6

A brown wooden sign read WELCOME TO SHADY BEND LAKE. Jack slowed the car and gazed over at Sara, noticing the rosy color had returned to her cheeks.

"Is this where you live?" she asked, swiveling her head left and right. She clutched her tote bag on her lap like a security blanket.

"Yes, we are almost there." Jack turned right, into a heavily wooded area.

Towering ponderosa pines reached high toward the sky, surrounding the empty, single lane road. While the posted speed limit was twenty-five miles per hour, the cracked asphalt, littered with potholes, forced them to drive slower.

A mile down the road they passed a small general store. A red and white CLOSED sign hung crookedly in the window, the area appearing deserted. Sara soon felt the forest closing in all around her.

"You didn't tell me you lived in the woods," she said.

Smiling, Jack ran his finger along the door panel and pushed a button. The windows lowered, and crisp, cool air circled into the car. Sara reached in her duffle bag for her cardigan sweater and wrapped it around her shoulders.

"I hope you packed something heavier. That flimsy thing is not going to keep you warm at night," he said.

"I have a few sweaters and my fleece jacket."

"Apparently you are not thinking clearly, it is much colder here. We will go shopping and buy you a warm wool coat."

Jack pulled over to the edge of the road to allow an oncoming car to pass. Lifting his fingers from the wheel, he waved and nodded at the dark-haired woman driving a silver Volvo.

As they drove a bit further, the road began to curve, snaking around the lake. A few houses set back from the road peeked out from behind the dense trees.

"How many people live here?" she asked.

"Twenty-one homes encircle the lake. It is a private community. Only a few people live here year round. Most are summer residents only."

After circling the lake, they reached the end of the road and Jack turned left, down a long, gravel driveway. Two signs, PRIVATE and DO NOT ENTER were nailed to the trunk of a tree. At the end of the driveway stood a large, rustic, cabin-style home surrounded and fenced in by tall aspen, fir, and spruce trees. Jack parked in front of the three-car garage doors. He exited the Cadillac and opened the passenger-side door.

With a sweeping wave of his hand and a slight bow of his head, he announced, "Welcome to the lake house."

Stepping out of the car, Sara slung her tote bag over her shoulder and gazed upon the secluded two-story house. Jack grabbed her suitcase and duffle bag and strutted along the broken stone walkway to the front door. Sara trailed behind him, dried leaves crunching underfoot as she observed the overgrown shrubbery in the yard.

Jack unlocked the iron padlock on the carved wooden door and motioned to Sara to enter the house. She walked inside and stood in the open foyer, gazing all around. It was not what she had pictured in her mind. She was surrounded by wood, everywhere. Dark wooden flooring, wood-paneled walls, and exposed beam ceilings.

Jack ambled past her, placing her luggage at the foot of the stairs.

"May I get you something to drink?" he asked. "A glass of water or perhaps some orange juice?"

"Water, please, thank you." She stood as still as a statue.

"Take a look around Sara, make yourself at home," he said as he headed toward the kitchen. "If you like, I can give you the grand tour in a moment or two."

Sara slowly made her way to the main living area.

Looking past the tired old furniture, she could see a view of the lake. As she walked over to the large picture window, she almost tripped on the edge of the frayed oriental rug in front of the massive rock fireplace.

Standing in front of the window, she was drawn to the shimmering blue tranquil waters, magnetized. The glistening lake, bordered by evergreen trees and high rolling mountains brought a much-needed sense of calm to her nerves. But her moment of peace lasted less than a minute.

In the background, she heard the sounds of cupboards opening and closing and dishes clanking. Jack soon paraded out of the kitchen holding a tarnished silver tray full of cheese and crackers, fruit, and beverages.

"Care to join me out on the deck?" He grinned at her and then turned, walking toward a large glass door off the kitchen area. Sara followed him.

"Here, let me open that for you," she reached for the handle.

"Just a minute, please, I need to unlock it. Hold this for me, will you?" Jack passed her the tray. He slid a key from his pocket and unlocked the handle and two deadbolts. He opened the door and they stepped outside onto the deck.

Sara placed the tray on a splintered wooden picnic table. Jack reached for a cup of tea and set it in front of her. The teacup had a large chip on the rim.

"Let us enjoy a little snack before dinner, shall we?"

"Thank you." She sat on the edge of the bench and carefully took a sip of tea.

Jack picked up a sprig of grapes, plucking off one after another, gobbling them as he paced back and forth on the deck.

"It sure is quiet here," she said, gazing toward the lake.

"Yes, it is very quiet and peaceful. One can only hear the chirping of birds, the quacking of ducks, and the echoes of one's mind."

Sara refocused her eyes on the backyard, noticing a weathered dock stretching out into the lake.

"Is that yours?" she asked, pointing to a small motorboat bobbing in the water and tethered at the end of the dock.

"Yes, it is. We will go for a cruise later. Now, finish your tea, it is time for the grand tour."

She placed the cups and dishes on the tray and carried it back inside, following Jack to the kitchen.

"Set that on the counter, above the dishwasher," he ordered.

Sara took a quick gander around the kitchen. *More wood.* The dark wooden cabinets were scratched and marred. Three rows of shelving were filled with mismatched dishes, cloudy crystal glassware, and a variety of spices. The rusty-ringed sink and grimy granite countertop were in dire need of a good scrubbing. The house stank, reeking of a stale, musty dampness mixed with the smell of onions. The stench made her nose twitch.

"Sara, my dear, come now, I am starting the tour."

She quickly made her way to the foyer where Jack was standing.

"Now, ahead of us, as you already know, we have the living room. Notice the way the natural light pours in from the windows. When you reach my age, you will appreciate the extra lighting. The piano in the corner was a gift for my wife. Oh, how I used to love to listen to her play. The rug you almost tripped on is a family heirloom; it belonged to my grandfather. I myself have stumbled on that rug many times and when I do, it is reminding me to watch my step." Waving his index finger in front of her face, he turned and walked away.

With lines forming between her eyebrows, she followed him.

"And here we have my absolute favorite room, the study."

Upon entering the room, her heart skipped a beat. Mounted on the wall was a huge brown moose head with enormous antlers. Its black beady eyes were staring directly at her.

"Please tell me that's fake," she winced, pointing to the wall.

"No, I am afraid not. But if it makes you feel any better, I did not shoot it; my father did."

Looking away, Sara bit down on the inside of her cheek and blinked back tears. She loved animals…all animals, big and small. She couldn't imagine how anyone could kill such a creature of nature. Swallowing the hard lump in her throat, she moved toward an antique bookcase that took up half of the wall.

"Ah, my Victorian bookcase," Jack came up behind her. Running his hand along the shelf, dust particles flurried in the air. "It is hand-carved mahogany. Notice the intricate design on the pilasters; it matches the trim on my desk."

Sara's gaze fell upon the double pedestal desk in the middle of the room. On top of it sat an older model computer. She pictured Jack sitting at his desk, online, playing cards. She then caught sight of a burgundy leather chair. Riddled with scratches and tears, shredded foam poked through the cracks.

Jack turned away and headed toward the kitchen. Sara trekked behind him.

"Here we have the dining area."

A rectangular wooden table with ladder-back chairs filled the space. In the center of the table sat a glass vase filled with orange lilies, red carnations, and yellow chrysanthemums. The flowers added a touch of color to the otherwise lackluster room. Stopping for a moment, she leaned in to smell them as Jack moved into the small kitchen.

"Once again, we have the kitchen. Make yourself at home, feel free to cook and prepare meals whenever you are hungry. Behind here is the pantry." He knocked on the door as he passed by it. "Inside you will find all the food and supplies you need."

Sara glanced at him and nodded.

"Now, let us head upstairs so you can select your room."

Jack walked back to the foyer, grabbing her luggage and carrying it up the stairs. Pausing at the top, he looked down over the staircase and called out to Sara.

"I said it is time to choose your room, my dear," he bellowed.

Sara marched up the stairs, her footfalls heavy on the creaky steps. *If he calls me 'dear' one more time, I swear I'm going to...*

"Oh, there you are. Now come this way, we have four rooms to choose from." She followed him as he turned left down a long narrow hallway.

"Here we have a small room with bunk beds; it is a bit cramped and not your style. Over here we have another room, but it tends to be dark...it only has one window. Now these two rooms here, both are appropriate. They share a connecting bathroom." Jack walked into the last room on the right. "I believe they call this setup a Jack-and-Jill; however, I do not know anyone named Jill and I have never used this bathroom," he snickered.

Sara didn't laugh at his silly joke as she stepped inside and peeked around the corner to check out the bathroom.

"I say you choose this room. It has a little sitting area that will suit you nicely." He set her luggage down at the foot of the bed.

She walked around the sparsely decorated bedroom,

giving it a quick once-over. Two large windows afforded abundant light and expansive views of the lake. An aqua blue and lavender patchwork quilt adorned the full-sized bed, and two mismatched throw pillows took the place of a headboard.

A solid oak wardrobe stood in the corner, and a small wooden chair with a crocheted fringe blanket draped over it was placed near the window. An Aztec tapestry hung on the wall, and a small figurine of three owls perched on a branch sat atop a wooden nightstand.

"What do you think?" Jack stood in the doorway with his hands on his hips.

Placing her tote bag on the chair, she gazed out the window toward the backyard.

"This room has a nice view of the lake. It'll be fine."

"Wonderful. Now feel free to unwind and unpack. I have placed some clean towels in the bathroom for you. Perhaps you would like to freshen up a bit."

He glanced at his watch and then back at Sara.

"It is four thirty-five. Dinner will be served promptly at five o'clock." Jack smiled wide and closed the door behind him.

7

Sara unzipped her duffle bag, pulled out her cosmetic case, and lined up her toiletries on the bathroom vanity. She stared into the dirty, spotted mirror and turned on the faucet. Water slowly streamed out into the rust-stained sink. After splashing cool water on her face, she reached for the folded towel. As she patted her face dry, she sniffed at the towel and crinkled her nose.

Eww, gross, it's mildewy. This towel stinks, the house smells...clearly Jack needs help here. This place desperately needs a thorough cleaning.

She soon heard the sounds of pots and pans clanging and music playing as she made her way downstairs. When she approached the dining area, she noticed the table was set. A white envelope with her name in blue-inked script lay alongside one of the plates. A bottle of red wine stood next to the vase of flowers.

"Hope you are hungry. I have made a special welcoming meal for you."

"That is very kind of you," she said, catching a strong whiff of garlic with a hint of tomato.

"It is our favorite, spaghetti with marinara."

"Oh?" *Since when is spaghetti 'our' favorite?*

"Well, I wanted you to feel at home." He gazed over at her. "I do hope you will be comfortable here."

Sara watched as he flitted about the kitchen.

"I figured on our first night we could become acquainted and plan out the week ahead of us. I am getting low on supplies, so perhaps we will go shopping tomorrow for groceries and such for the tournament."

"Sure, that's why I'm here. To help you, right?"

"Yes, indeed, it is help I need." He chuckled. "Now have a seat, dinner is served."

Sara tugged at the rickety wooden chair and sat down. Jack appeared over her shoulder holding pasta tongs and dropped thickly coated spaghetti onto her plate. She leaned back to avoid being splattered with the bright red sauce. Walking around the table, he piled a generous serving onto his plate and sat across from her. He reached for the wine, twisted off the cap, and held up the bottle.

"Care for some?" he asked. "It is not real wine but non-alcoholic called Berry Blended something or other."

"Sure, why not." Forcing a smile, she lifted her glass.

Pouring the dark, fruity drink into her glass, he filled it to the rim. She took a quick sip and lowered the glass, pursing her lips. *Ooh, that's tart.* She ate some of the pasta and placed her fork on her dish.

"Do you not like it?" he asked, talking with his mouth full, sauce dribbling from his lips.

"It's good." She blotted the corner of her mouth with her napkin, hoping he'd notice and do the same. "It's a little heavy on the garlic for my taste, but good."

"I eat lots of garlic," his eyes widened, "keeps the demons away."

Demons, Sara wondered but didn't ask.

The look in his eyes was daunting. The dim lighting not only made his eyes appear darker, but something about them troubled her. Jack devoured his pasta, washing it down with two more glasses of the faux red wine.

"Ready to go for our sunset cruise?" he asked. "The lake is spectacular at this time of day."

"Okay, I'll help clear the dishes."

"Not right now, they can wait. But before we go, open your envelope."

Sara reached for the envelope, unfolded the flap, and pulled out a handful of hundred dollar bills.

"That is your buy-in money, as promised, three thousand dollars."

"Thank you so much. Thank you for the opportunity; I appreciate it."

"Now, go put on your warmest sweater and meet me outside on the deck." Pushing back his chair, he stood up and walked over to the door. He lifted his jacket from the coat hook.

Sara felt guilty leaving the dirty plates. As soon as Jack went outside, she quickly cleared the table, washed the dishes and put them away. She went upstairs and set the envelope of money on the nightstand. She grabbed her fleece jacket out of her suitcase, slipped it on, and then jogged down the hallway and rushed down the stairs.

Outside, at the end of the dock, Jack was standing by the boat. Sara walked out onto the deck, skipping down the steps to the backyard. Jack raised his arm, waving to her.

The dilapidated wooden planks creaked beneath her feet as she walked toward him. Nearing the end, she slowed her gait. She took long strides, careful not to trip in the areas of the broken or missing planks. Reaching out his hand, he helped her climb aboard and then untied the boat.

"Just in time, look around you," he said. "The colors are fantastic."

As the evening sun colored the clouds and sky, the rippling waters glimmered with hues of hot pink and deep purple.

"Wow, it's stunning," she said. "Purple is my favorite color."

"Mine, too. Now sit back and enjoy. The air is free."

Sara took a seat and gazed all around her. "It's beautiful here, and so serene."

"Yes, it is. I will never understand why anyone would ever want to leave." Sitting behind the wheel, Jack stared into the waters as he steered the boat around the lake.

"Sara, I want to thank you again for accepting my offer. I feel confident I have chosen the right girl this time."

"This time?" she asked, her forehead wrinkling.

"Well, to be honest, a few others have tried to help me here at the lake house, but I gather this type of setting is not for everyone. It is not your average cup of tea."

"What do you mean?" she asked, a slight tremor in her voice.

"Some of the girls had a difficult time with the remoteness; others, I assume, had a hard time with me." He paused. "Being so isolated, well, it can mess with your head." Raising his hand, he tapped his temple with a finger.

"How long have you lived here?"

"I have been here for years…many, many years. But it has not been the same since…well, after my wife…"

"I'm sorry, what about your wife?"

"I prefer not to talk about it right now. Perhaps another time."

In awkward silence, they slowly circled the forest-ringed lake. As dusk strengthened, Jack grew tired, and the boat puttered along. Darkness fell as they returned home, guided only by the blue LED lights under the boat.

After reaching the dock, Sara hopped out while Jack secured the boat.

"Wait for me, please," he said. "This old dock is in desperate need of repair. I do not want you tripping or worse, falling through."

"Okay."

"Here, hold on," he offered her his arm.

Side by side, they traipsed along the loose planks toward the house. Two lines of solar landscape lights formed a pathway through the backyard to the deck area. Once inside, Jack double locked the back door.

"It has been a long day for me, time to rest these old bones. Tomorrow is Sunday. What do you say we go out for breakfast? My treat, then we will shop for groceries."

"Sounds like a plan. What time were you thinking?"

"Can you be ready to leave by nine?"

"Yes.

"Well, then, good night, Sara. Sleep tight and do not let the pesky bed bugs bite."

8

"What on earth were you thinking?"

"What did I do now?"

"Why is she here?"

"To help with the tournament."

"The tournament?"

"Yes, the poker tournament next weekend, she is here for the week to help me organize."

"Organize? Is that what it's called?"

"What is that supposed to mean?"

"Never mind. She won't even last the week."

"Why do you make things so difficult?"

"Because it's what I do."

"Apparently."

"I bet she's just like all the others."

"No, she is not."

"How much?"

"How much what?"

"How much you want to bet she is?"

"Please stop. I have no time for games."

"Since when don't you have time for games? All you ever do is play games."

"Look, just give her a chance before you pass judgment. I think she is special, very special."

"I'll give her a chance. When are you going to introduce me to her?"

"Not yet, it is much too soon, let her settle in first. You tend to come on a bit too strong at times."

9

The bright morning sun streamed through the windows, lighting up the entire room. Sara had forgotten to close the curtains before she went to bed. She had just awakened when she heard a faint knock on the bedroom door. Squinting her eyes, she rolled over, reaching for her watch on the nightstand, 8:03 a.m.

"Sara, my dear, are you awake?" Jack called out from behind the door.

"Yes, I'll be down shortly."

Once out of bed, she took a quick shower. As she toweled off and dressed, she could hear music blaring, the sound carrying throughout the house.

Sara was not a morning person, unable to function until coffee flowed through her veins. The loud music soon began pulsating inside her head. She lumbered down the stairs and headed toward the kitchen, following the smell of freshly brewed coffee.

"Good morning, I made us some dark roast," Jack handed her a steaming cup.

"Thank you," she said, cradling the mug in her hands.

"Not sure how you take it. The sugar and creamers are over there."

Three different flavors of coffee creamers were lined up on the counter: French vanilla, hazelnut, and pumpkin spice.

"The hazelnut is my favorite." He watched as she tasted her coffee.

Sara picked up the French vanilla, read the ingredients and decided to pass. Instead, she lifted the lid of the pint-sized glass sugar bowl, plunked two cubes of sugar in her cup and gave the coffee a quick stir.

"Did you rest well?" Raising his cup, he slurped his coffee.

"It took me a while to fall asleep."

"When you sleep in a strange place, it is always hard the first night. It will get better, I promise." He grinned.

Sara sipped her coffee while Jack went into the living room to turn the volume down on the stereo. As her stomach absorbed the caffeine, her ears and head were thankful to hear the thumping sounds fade away. Noticing Jack's cup was empty, she rinsed it and wiped away the sticky mess he'd left on the countertop.

When she put the creamers back in the refrigerator, she

eyed the yellow smiley face magnet on the front of the door. It
held a small piece of paper with the words 'shopping list'
written on it. Pulling the paper off the fridge, she began
searching through the drawers. Jack returned to the kitchen.

"Are you looking for something?"

"Yes, a pen. I want to add a few things to the shopping
list."

Jack reached on top of the fridge for his ballpoint pen,
clicked it and handed it to her. She scrawled a few items on
the paper.

"What can I add to the list for you?"

"I already have my list. I hung that paper there to remind
me to shop. It is time to go."

Folding the paper in half, she tucked it inside her tote bag
and followed him out the door.

Outside, a cool, swift breeze blew the scent of pine
through the morning air. Sara breathed deeply, cleansing her
lungs, trying to expel the stale air she had inhaled indoors.
Stepping through dead leaves and broken twigs, they
approached the Cadillac parked in the driveway. Jack
unlocked the doors, and they climbed inside.

The car cruised along the long narrow road that curved
through the trees, hugging the lake. They didn't pass a single
soul. The road was deserted.

After a twenty-minute drive to the center of town, they
arrived at the Sugar Bear Diner located on the main road. In
front was a statue of a big brown bear wearing a pink apron.

Jack pulled into the diner's small parking lot crammed with vehicles.

"Looks like a busy place," she said.

"It is the most popular breakfast joint in town."

Jack wedged the Cadillac into a tight spot next to a tree, not giving Sara much room to climb out. She opened the door and had to turn sideways to squeeze out of the car.

The bell above the door jingled as they entered the diner. Jack walked over and slid into the first booth by the window. Sara scooted in across from him as a frantic, heavyset waitress rushed over to them, wearing the same pink apron as the bear out front.

"Good morning," the waitress said in a hoarse voice, sliding two plastic-covered menus in front of them. "Give me a few and I'll be back to take your order."

Sara read the top line of the menu out loud. "Home of the six stack pancakes." Her eyes grew wide as she studied the picture of six thick pancakes, dripping with syrup and topped with mounds of whipped cream.

"Want to share an order?" he asked. "Three for you and three for me."

"That is half my caloric intake for the day."

"Oh come on, live a little. I have seen you eat, pecking at your food like a darn bird."

"I guess I can be a little bad. It is Sunday, after all."

"Well, if eating pancakes makes you bad, I could be bad every day," he wiggled his eyebrows.

The waitress returned to take their order. "Now, what can I get you two?" she asked, out of breath.

"We will split a six stack, along with a cup of coffee for me and a glass of orange juice for the young lady."

Picking up the menus, the waitress hustled away.

"Hope you do not mind me ordering for you. I remembered how much you like orange juice."

"No problem, I already had my caffeine fix for the day. I feel jittery if I drink more than one cup."

"So tell me, what is on that shopping list of yours?"

"Soy milk for my coffee and a few cleaning supplies. I figured, when we return, I could maybe dust and vacuum, straighten up the house a little."

"I do apologize for the house being in such disarray. As I told you, I am a bit behind on things. I had a housekeeper for a few months but had to let her go."

"Why?"

"She was stealing from me."

"Oh no, I'm sorry to hear that."

"Yes, well, those things can happen when you deal with different types of people."

"Well, I hope you know you don't have to worry about me."

"That is all well and good, but as the saying goes…"

"What saying?"

"One can never really know one's true intentions."

Looking down at the table, Sara gathered her thoughts. "If

you don't mind me asking, what happened at the last tournament? You mentioned there was some type of incident."

"Well, let us see." Placing his elbows on the table, he steepled his hands. "At the last tournament, there was a gal who helped me…Sheila was her name. Unfortunately, she disappeared one day."

"Disappeared? What do you mean disappeared?" Her eyebrows pressed together.

"One day she went out and never returned."

"Never returned?" she gasped.

Holding her gaze, he snapped his fingers. "Gone. Poof. Vanished into thin air."

Sara's eyes and mouth froze wide open.

A moment later the waitress reappeared with their breakfast and set the dish of pancakes between them. Reaching into her apron, she pulled out a handful of creamers and placed them in front of Jack.

"Anything else for you two?" she asked, setting an extra plate on the table.

"No, we are good, thank you." Jack winked at her and she rushed away. "Thoughtful lady, she always remembers my extra cream."

Tearing the lids off five mini-creamers, Jack lined them up in a row and reached for his spoon. As he poured each creamer into his coffee, he stirred vigorously, the spoon clanking against the cup. After taking a few sips, he started whistling while he stacked the empty plastic containers on top of each other.

She could sense he was becoming agitated and figured it would be best to change the subject. "Do you come here often?" she asked, trying to keep her voice steady.

"As a matter of fact, I do. Their breakfast is dee-licious."

Sara looked around, glancing at the other diners as if searching for an answer. Gazing past Jack's shoulder, she focused her eyes on the woman in the booth behind them. She had curly gray hair and wore a bright marigold sweater that looked as though she had knitted it herself.

The woman, who was facing Sara, kept looking up and over at her while tapping her lips with her forefinger. Sara wondered if the woman was a regular customer like Jack.

Maybe the woman had seen this girl Sheila. Maybe, at one time, Sheila sat in the same booth, in the exact seat as she was sitting. Maybe the woman knew what happened to Sheila. Maybe she had the answer.

Sara watched closely as Jack stabbed at the pancakes with his fork. Sliding his knife horizontally through the middle of the stack, he moved the top three pancakes onto the smaller plate, pushing the bigger plate in front of Sara.

"Dig in," he commanded, pointing at her with the knife.

10

After breakfast, they drove a mile down the road to Redfield's Market. In front of the store, Jack reached for a shopping cart, wheeled it over to Sara, and then went back to grab another one.

"Want to race?" he asked, pushing a cart with a wonky wheel.

Sara gave him a side-eyed look of exasperation.

"I am joking, we have lots of groceries to buy; we need to stock up."

When they entered the store, a large display of autumn decorations captured Sara's attention. Various arrangements of gold and orange flowers, harvest wreaths, and scented candles graced the tables. Cardboard boxes filled with all sizes of pumpkins sat on the floor.

"Would you like some fresh flowers for your room?" he asked. "You can pick whatever you want."

Sara chose a small bouquet and then reached for a candle, placing them in her cart. Turning back to the display, she bent down and picked up a large pumpkin.

"We can paint a face on it and put it outside the front door." She smiled.

"Well, if you must. If it will make you happy, go ahead and get it." He rolled his cart away.

Sara followed, pushing her cart behind him. She watched as he dodged customers, zigzagging up and down the aisles, putting two of each item into his cart. When they reached the dairy section, he stopped short.

"Is this your milk?" he asked, pointing to a quart of skim milk.

"No, that's not it; I hope to find it." Gazing at the signs above the aisle, she looked for the 'household items' section. *There it is…aisle four.*

"Jack, I'm going to get the cleaning supplies. I'll meet you up front in a few, okay?"

Whirling her cart around, she headed down aisle four. As she was checking off the items on her list, she heard her name being paged over the store's intercom.

"Sara Tyler, please report to the courtesy desk, Sara Tyler."

What the heck? Why are they paging me?

Gripping the handle of the shopping cart, she raced to the

front of the store. When she located the 'customer service' desk, Jack was there, standing next to an overflowing cart. He had his arms folded across his chest. As she rolled her cart toward him, he unfolded his arms and threw his hands up in despair.

"Where did you go? I have been looking all over for you," he scolded her. People in the nearest checkout lines were looking at them.

"I told you. I went to find the cleaning supplies. I was only gone a few minutes."

"You cannot simply wander off like that," he said, stomping his foot. "I thought something happened to you. I turned around and you had disappeared." His eyes glistened.

"I'm sorry, please don't be upset." She edged in closer to comfort him, "I thought you heard me tell you." Looking into his eyes, she noticed one of his pupils was larger than the other. He drew his handkerchief from his pocket and wiped away a tear trickling down his cheek.

Jack's face was full of fear and agony. He looked lost, abandoned. Sara had sensed something much deeper was causing his pain.

It hurt Sara to see anyone alone. Whenever she saw someone alone at a restaurant, alone in the world, she felt sadness. Deep down, maybe Sara feared she, too, would end up alone.

Six months after her father passed away, she had lost her job. Still mourning the unexpected loss of her dad, it had sent her into a mild depression. When she lost her job, she lost touch with her coworkers and became more and more isolated from her small circle of friends. While she visited her mother twice a month, her mom's failing health would depress her even more. Most of the time, she kept to herself, holed up inside her apartment, alone.

"Are you ready to go? Did you find everything you need?" she asked, rearranging the two, twelve-roll packs of paper towels about to fall from Jack's cart.

"Yes, I need to return home," he grumbled, "the game starts soon."

Back at the house, Sara stood in the huge, walk-in pantry putting the groceries away while Jack retreated to the living room. As he settled in front of the TV, relaxing in his leather recliner, loud roars and ear-piercing whistles of a football game made their way into the kitchen area.

While she stacked the newly purchased cans of soup and packaged foods, she observed rows and rows of the same items. He had plenty of food already stored. The top shelves alone held endless bundles of paper goods. He had enough supplies to last for months.

Sara turned to walk out of the pantry and bumped right into Jack, his sudden appearance startling her.

"Ooh," she jumped back a step, "I didn't know you were there."

"I need to go out. Will you be okay here?"

"Yes, I'll be fine. I finished putting everything away and was just about ready to clean the house."

"Very well, be back in an hour or so." Reaching into his pocket, Jack pulled out his keys and disappeared out the back door.

Sara wondered where he'd rushed off to so quickly. He had been quiet ever since the little episode at the store. But she welcomed a break from him. It would provide a chance to vacuum without interrupting his game and also give her some much-needed breathing room.

After putting on a pair of rubber gloves, she started scrubbing down the kitchen. She then swept the dining area, dusted and vacuumed the living room, and proceeded to the study. She dreaded going in that room; she hated the way she felt in there. She could sense a dark energy as soon as she entered. She figured it had something to do with the bodiless animal on the wall that was once again staring at her.

"Hello Mr. Moose," she said, gazing into his eyes. "You deserved to live. I'm so sorry they killed you—murdered you in cold blood."

She figured if she acknowledged the animal's presence, dead or alive, she could comfortably share the room with him.

Sara went about dusting the bookshelves, Jack's desk, and

a long wooden table against the wall. In the middle of the table sat a large color printer. Surrounding it were stacks of papers, empty folders, and three-ring binders. She was careful not to disturb any of the documents as she quickly reorganized them.

In the corner of the room stood a small writing desk. It didn't seem to belong with the other furniture. It stuck out like a sore thumb among all the other dark masculine décor.

The unfinished wooden desk with matching chair had a more modern design. It was similar to the desk in her apartment, which she'd bought when she redecorated except hers was painted white. Pulling out the chair, she sat down for a minute to rest her aching back.

When she ran her cloth across the desk, it snagged on the handle of the top drawer. A loose thread had become tangled around the knob. She gently tugged on the cloth to release it. The drawer opened. Inside was a small laptop computer she studied for a few seconds. She picked up the dust cloth and closed the drawer.

Gathering the broom and bucket full of cleaning products, she headed up to the second floor. At the top of the stairs, off to the right, was a door. She guessed it to be Jack's room, the master bedroom. It was separate from the other bedrooms that shared the hallway to the left. It was the only room he didn't show her on his tour of the house. Walking over to the door, she turned the handle. It was locked.

That's one less room to clean.

She continued down the hall, spruced up all the bedrooms

and scrubbed down the bathroom. After she had finished
sweeping, she took a break and flopped on the bed in her
room, worn out from the day's activities. The mattress springs
creaked when she moved as she tried to find comfort.

As she nodded off, a loud slamming noise jolted her. She
quickly got up and peeked out the window. The wind had
picked up, blowing through the trees and rustling the leaves.
She searched the backyard and then lowered her gaze to the
deck area by the back door. *I must be hearing things.*

As she walked back over to the bed, she stubbed her toe
on the edge of her suitcase. She hadn't fully unpacked her
luggage still sitting on the floor against the wall. *No time
like the present.* When she opened the free-standing
wardrobe, two metal hangers dangled from the wooden rod.
*Two hangers won't be enough. I'll need a few more
than that.*

Meandering through the bathroom, she opened the door to
the adjoining bedroom. The room was furnished similar to
hers but had a slightly larger wardrobe. It also contained a full
length, standing Cheval mirror. She had admired the antique
piece earlier when she had cleaned it.

As she passed by the mirror, the late afternoon sun
streamed through the window, highlighting a few spots she
had missed. She pulled her shirt sleeve over her wrist and
began to wipe away the streaks. The mirror swung back in its
frame. Reaching out with both hands to straighten it, she tilted
it toward her and caught her reflection. She screamed, nearly

jumping out of her skin. Through the mirror, she saw Jack standing in the doorway behind her.

"What are you doing in here?" he asked, glaring at her with predatory eyes. His fists were clenching and unclenching at his sides.

"I-I was looking for hangers. I-I finished cleaning and there was a spot I missed...on the mirror." Her heart hammered against her ribs as she caught her breath. "You scared the hell out of me."

"Oops," he said. Smirking, he walked toward her. "By the way, you did a great job on the house today." He threw two hundred dollar bills on the bed.

"What's that for?" she asked, lifting her hand to her chest.

"For cleaning the house; I appreciate the extra effort. Extra efforts shall be rewarded."

And just as quickly as he appeared, he disappeared again.

11

Walking around the study, Jack paused to inspect the long table against the wall. The papers were stacked in neat piles, and the folders and binders stood upright in a row. As he turned back toward his desk, he narrowed his eyes. Suspended by chains, the bronze, pine cone weights of the cuckoo clock hung inches from the floor. The clock had stopped.

Sara came tromping down the stairs, looking for Jack. When she poked her head in the study, she saw him tinkering with the clock.

"Do you need any help?"

"No, I am trying to start this darn clock again. It quits on me all the time."

"I was going to heat up some soup for dinner. Would you like some?"

"Yes, I will only be a few more minutes in here."

Sara went into the kitchen, grabbed a can of soup from the pantry and lit the gas stove. As she stood at the stove stirring a pot of vegetable soup, she admired the clean kitchen. Although weary and sore after cleaning all day, she was proud of the results.

She reached to the shelf above her and found the candle she had put there earlier. As she held it to her nose, she inhaled the fragrant scent of apple and spice. Lowering her hand, she lit the candle's wick from the flame on the stove and placed it on the counter. She was hoping it would mask the musty odor still lingering in the air.

After spooning the heated soup into two bowls, she arranged a row of salted crackers on a dish. She set the food on the dining table and heard the cuckoo clock chime eight times. Jack walked over and took a seat.

"What is that I smell? Did you bake me an apple pie?" His jaw dropped.

"No, sorry, it's the candle I bought at the store."

"That is too bad, I love apple pie." He pouted in disappointment.

"I can make one for you tomorrow if you'd like."

"No, tomorrow we need to begin preparations for the tournament. There will be no time for baking. Perhaps I will buy one at the bakery the next time I go to town."

Scooping up a handful of crackers, he crushed them in his fist, the crumbled pieces falling into his bowl. Gazing at her, he slurped his soup, licking his lips. Sara ate small spoonfuls while looking down at the table.

"Is everything okay?" he asked, wiping the corners of his mouth with his fingers.

"Yeah, I'm fine. I'm a little tired."

"Well then, you better go upstairs to bed. Tomorrow we start at seven o'clock. We have much to do before our guests arrive, we have a busy week ahead of us."

"I'll be up and ready."

"In the study, there is a small desk. You may have already seen it. That will be your work station. You will find a computer inside the top drawer. It is yours to use while here."

"Okay, thank you." Sara arose from her seat, cleared the table and washed the dishes.

Jack moseyed into the living room and turned on the television. Easing himself back in his recliner with his remote, he clicked through the channels and settled on a movie. The sounds of galloping horses and gunshots soon echoed through the house.

As Sara walked past the living room heading toward the stairs, she caught a glimpse of an old black-and-white Western on TV.

Upstairs, on her way to her room, she passed the adjoining bedroom and stopped. Hesitating for a few seconds, she took a step back and then entered. *I never did find those hangers I was searching for earlier.* She twisted the handle on the wardrobe. *Locked. Another locked door.* She sighed. She was too tired to deal with it.

Every single muscle in her body ached; she was sore and fatigued. It had taken her over six hours to clean his house. She was used to her tiny apartment that took less than forty minutes. It was always clean because she couldn't stand living in a dirty house; clutter and disorder drove her nuts. She told herself she would not be driven crazy by Jack's messy house and accepted the fact she would be cleaning up after him all week.

When she went into the bathroom to get ready for bed, she gazed at the sparkling clean, jetted tub. *Oh, how a massage would help my aching back.* But the thought of sitting in water, exposed and vulnerable in a stranger's house made her uncomfortable.

She walked to the door that connected with the adjoining bedroom and locked it. Turning around, she went to the bathroom door connecting to her bedroom. There was no lock on it. *Well, that figures. The door that needs a lock doesn't have one.* She stared into the tub for a moment. *Since he's watching a movie, I should be okay.*

Sara drew the bath water, pouring in a capful of shampoo, then rolled up a large bath towel and placed it within arm's reach. She undressed and stepped into the warm water. The switch for the bubble-making air jets wouldn't work. Despite the fact that it was broken, she leaned back and tried to relax anyway.

A few minutes later, she heard a doorknob turn. She immediately sat up and grabbed the towel.

"Sara, are you okay in there?" Jack called out from behind the bathroom door.

"Yes, I'm fine. I'm getting ready for bed," she replied while standing in the tub, holding the towel wrapped around her.

"It is time to sleep, a chance to dream," he spoke in a whispery voice.

"Good night, Jack," she said.

Walking away, he didn't hear her.

Sara drained the tub, put on her pajamas, and crawled into bed. While her body yearned for rest, her mind refused to stop racing. Her thoughts were scattered. She lay there, staring at the ceiling, second-guessing her decision in accepting Jack's offer. Something didn't feel right. There was something about Jack about which she was unsure, something she couldn't quite understand. Something about him was off.

He seemed friendly and accommodating, for the most part. However, something about him put her on edge, the way he leered at her with a strange, glassed-over look in his eyes. He was secretive and distant regarding his personal life. He had started to tell her about his wife but hadn't mentioned anything about children. He hadn't told her the work he does for a living either, the type of job he does, or did.

The way he throws money around, and all the hundred dollar bills. Whatever he does, he must do well for himself. In time, she thought, *maybe he will be more open with me.* Being a private person herself, she wasn't one to pry.

The glow of the moon through the window reminded her once again she had forgotten to close the curtains. Climbing out of bed, she went over to the large panes of glass.

A strong gust of wind swept through the backyard, stirring up leaves and swaying the trees. Sara could hear its whistling howl; its force rattled the windows. She peered out into the darkness, in the direction of the lake. Only its outline was visible, an ominous black silhouette.

This place looks so different at night. It even feels different. Her gaze followed the trail of solar lights back to the yard and to the deck below. A sudden movement caught her eye.

She placed her hands on the glass, fingers splayed, and strained to take a closer look. A tree branch slapped against the window. Jumping back, she let out an unsteady breath. Her heart raced. The branch kept smacking and scraping the window while the wind continued to blow.

Sara quickly closed the curtains and climbed into bed. Pulling the covers up to her neck, her eyes remained open, scanning the pitch dark room. She didn't have the chance to dream that night. She barely slept a wink.

"I almost forgot something."

"What?"

"Remember last night when I said I bet she's just like all the others?"

"Vaguely."

"Well, it's a good thing I didn't bet."

"Why?"

"Because I would have lost."

"Whatever are you talking about? You would have lost?"

"Yeah, I would have lost the bet."

"What makes you say that?"

"You were right. She's not like the others."

"I told you."

"But what you somehow failed to recognize was that she's crazy."

"How can you say that? You do not even know her."

"I saw her talking to the moose."

"What moose? Now you sound like the crazy one."

"The moose head on the wall. She walked right up to it, stared into its eyes, and talked to it. I saw her mouth move. It was comical at first, but then she looked so sad."

"Have you been spying on her? What else did she do?"

"Clean. She cleaned up the mess of papers in the study."

"Yes, I inspected everything. She did a great job too. Better than the last one."

"Speaking of the last one, what was her name again?"

"Sheila."

"That's right, has this one asked you about her yet?"

"Yes, actually she asked me about her today over breakfast."

"What did you tell her?"

"I told her the truth."

"The truth?"

"Yes, I told her she disappeared."

"You did? And she didn't even ask you how she disappeared?"

"We were conveniently interrupted."

"Hmm, so she doesn't know the whole story."

"No."

"And what happens when she finds out?"

"She will not find out. She must never find out."

"That's what you said the last time."

Sitting at his desk, Jack drummed his fingers, staring up at the clock, 7:25 a.m. Two minutes later, the sound of footfalls approached him from behind. He gazed over his shoulder.

"Well, good morning Miss Sleepy Head, you are late."

"Sorry, I hardly slept. I just fell asleep, like an hour or so ago."

Stifling a yawn, Sara walked over to the small desk. A cup of heavily creamed, lukewarm coffee, awaited her.

"Thank you for the coffee," she said, peeking into the cup.

"Hope you like it."

Jack poked around at his papers and then raised his eyes back to her. He watched as she sat down in the chair, opened the drawer, and pulled out the laptop computer. Sara felt him staring at her.

"So, what do you need me to work on today?" After taking a sip of coffee, she grimaced.

"I have finished writing your to-do list. Number one is to find a lighting contractor. I need to install lights in the backyard. At night you cannot see a thing."

"Yeah, I know," she whispered under her breath.

"What did you say?"

"I said, I know. You can't see anything at night...out back in the yard."

"How do you know?" Lowering his chin, he peered over the top of his reading glasses.

"Because when I went to close the curtains last night, I thought I saw someone...or something...in the backyard."

"Someone or something? Which one was it?"

"I'm not sure. It was so dark and windy. All kinds of leaves and twigs were blowing around."

"Well, I will be sure to keep my eyes peeled for someone or something." He chuckled.

Gazing at him, she shook her head.

"It is that time of year," he said. "The winds of change are starting to blow."

"I'll be right back."

Sara got up and traipsed to the kitchen. Tossing the overly sweet hazelnut-flavored coffee into the sink, she rinsed the cup and poured another, black, no sugar. She would have to make do without her soy milk, as the store didn't have any.

She took a sip of the dark, bitter brew and peered out the

kitchen window, sweeping her gaze over the back deck. As she raised the cup to her lips, she felt a hand on her shoulder and whirled around. The cup slipped through her fingers, shattering on the floor.

"You scared the living daylights out of me," she squealed.

Trembling, she reached for the paper towels and bent down to pick up the shards of ceramic. As she mopped up the spilled mess, she noticed Jack had swapped out his noisy cowboy boots for a pair of black rubber-soled shoes.

"Perhaps you should lay off the caffeine." Reaching for the pot, he poured the last of the coffee into his cup. "Come now, there is work to do," he said, and then walked away.

Fuming inside, she scowled. If her eyes could've shot daggers through his back, they would have. *No sleep and no coffee. It's going to be a long, miserable day.*

Jack played cards on his computer while Sara worked on her to-do list. She searched the internet for local contractors and sent out emails, requesting appointments. A few hours had passed when her cell phone vibrated on top of her desk. She didn't recognize the number.

"Hello," she answered.

"Hi, this is Ted Connor, Connor's Custom Lighting. I received an email requesting some pricing on outdoor lights. It said to call this number."

"Oh, yes. I emailed you, thanks for the quick reply." She looked over at Jack who was leering at her.

"What type of lights are you interested in?" Ted asked.

"I don't know. I mean...I don't know because the lights aren't for me, not for my house. I'm calling for my... " Sara glanced at Jack again and moved the phone to her other ear. "I'm calling for my boss."

'Boss' was the first word to enter her foggy, non-caffeinated mind. Jack apparently was pleased with the title from the smug look of delight on his face.

"Tomorrow morning at eight? Yes, that should work." Sara cradled the phone against her shoulder while scribbling on the notepad.

"Oh, yes, it is...hold on a second, please." Cupping her hand over the phone, she looked over at Jack. "What's the address here?"

"Twenty-one Shady Bend Road," he said, raising an eyebrow and shaking his head.

"Twenty-one Shady Bend Road," she repeated into the phone. "Okay, thank you and see you tomorrow."

Sara ended the call and opened the calendar application on her phone. After entering the eight o'clock appointment reminder, below the time slot she read the words, 'call Mom.' Gazing into her phone, she paused for a moment to think.

When did I last speak to her? Oh yeah, when I was waiting for my car. That was Friday. Today is...Monday. Ugh, I forgot to call her yesterday.

"What are you doing?" Jack's voice escalated.

"What do you mean? I'm doing what you asked me to

do…making these appointments. The light guy will be here tomorrow morning at eight."

"I have a landline phone here on my desk. You can use it to make your calls." Picking up the cordless handset, he walked over to her and plunked it on her desk.

She reached for the phone, looked it over, pressed a few buttons, and handed it back to him.

"It doesn't work. Maybe it needs a new battery." She turned to face the computer.

"Okay, Sara, take a break, it is almost lunch time. I have an errand to do in town and will return in a bit." He went to his desk, gathered his keys, and left the room.

Sara waited in the study until she heard the door close. She picked up her cell phone and called her mom.

"Good morning, Sun Meadows Assisted Care."

"Hi, Helen Tyler, please."

"One moment, let me transfer you."

The phone rang and rang. She was about to end the call when someone finally picked up.

"Hello," Helen sounded perturbed.

"Hi mom, I'm sorry I forgot to call you yesterday. I've been so busy with everything going on. I haven't been sleeping much and lost track of time."

"I'm getting ready to leave for lunch with Dorothy from next door."

"Well, I just wanted to check in and make sure you were doing okay."

"I'm good."

"Okay mom, love you."

"Be safe, wherever you are." Helen hung up.

Sara exhaled and leaned back in the chair, glancing up at the ornate wooden clock on the wall. Tick-tock, tick-tock, the pendulum swung back and forth, lulling her tired mind. Moments later, two miniature doors flew open. A tiny red bird poked its head out and cuckooed twelve times. Rolling her eyes, she headed to the kitchen.

After preparing a grilled cheese sandwich, she decided to eat outside on the deck. She was hoping some fresh air would cure her drowsiness. Holding the plate in one hand, she reached for the door handle but it wouldn't turn. She set the plate on the counter and tried the handle again, this time with both hands. *Is it stuck?* She gazed above to the deadbolt, requiring a key to unlock from the inside. She tried the handle one more time, but the door wouldn't open.

She marched out of the kitchen and headed toward the foyer. Holding onto the iron-levered handle on the front door, she gave it a strong pull. It didn't budge. Jack had locked her inside the house.

"Help!" Sara heard Jack call out. "I need some help over here."

Following his voice, she dashed from the study to the foyer. Jack was teetering in the entryway, balancing two large paper shopping bags in his arms. One of the bags was tearing open at the bottom. Sara put her hand under the ripped bag, taking it from him and carrying it to the kitchen.

"Thank you, we almost lost our pies."

"Pies?"

"Yes, I waited over two hours for them, they are freshly baked. The kind lady at the bakery made them especially for us. I figured we could try some different flavors and then order a few for the tournament."

"You were gone all day," she mentioned.

"Well, I told you, I had things to do. Is something wrong? You seem to be bothered."

"Speaking of 'fresh'…I wanted to eat lunch outside and breathe in some 'fresh' air. But you locked me inside this house…I couldn't get out."

"Sara, please, calm down. I locked the doors for your protection."

"Protection? Protection from what? From whom? The demons?" she asked, her voice shrill with sarcasm.

"I did not want anything to happen to you." He frowned, his eyes downcast.

"I'm a big girl, Jack, I can take care of myself."

"My dear, if you were in a position to take care of yourself, you would not be here now, would you?"

Furious, she turned and walked to the back door. Folding her arms in front of her chest she scanned the backyard, her gaze falling upon the deck. The pumpkin she had bought was under the picnic table.

"Am I allowed to go out and get my pumpkin?" she huffed.

"Why of course you are. Speaking of pumpkins, how does pumpkin pecan streusel sound?" Lifting the lids on the two pie boxes, he hesitated on which one to cut first.

"Sounds way too sweet."

"Well, I bought a double-crust apple, too, for us to share," he looked over at her with pleading eyes.

"Jack, listen. I'm sorry for raising my voice, for being upset. I'm just really tired."

"Then you need to go to bed early tonight and catch up on some sleep."

"Yeah, I know, but first I need some air."

Opening the door, Sara stepped onto the deck into the cool evening air. She took long deep breaths to help calm and quiet her mind. She walked over to the edge of the deck, went down the stairs, and through the backyard in the direction of the dock.

As the sun dipped below the hills along the horizon, the lake caught the setting rays. Glowing streaks of gold and orange glittered across the water's surface as the lake mirrored the sky above.

As she reached the end of the dock, she was greeted by a gentle breeze and the water lapping below. She perched herself on the edge of the dock, her legs dangling above the water. Sitting peacefully, she gazed into the glistening lake and savored the serenity.

A pair of ducks drifted past her on an evening swim. They broke her gaze as she watched them sail through the water, carried by the wind.

As the ducks glided across the water, beneath the waves of their trail, something caught her eye. It appeared to be floating upright, a few feet from the surface. Leaning over the edge, she stretched her neck out, trying to get a closer look. Off in the distance, someone was calling her name.

"Sara, Sara."

She stood up and turned around. Jack was standing in the backyard, waving his arms over his head.

The sun had set, and the air had grown colder. Sara felt a chill at the nape of her neck. Wrapping her arms tightly around her body, she walked carefully across the dock toward the house. When she reached the deck, she stooped down under the picnic table to pick up the pumpkin. Carrying it inside, she placed it on the dining room table.

"What were you doing out there?" Jack walked over holding two slices of apple pie and slid a plate in front of her.

"Oh, getting some fresh air. It's colder here at night."

"Winter will soon be upon us."

"Yeah well, I'll need to buy a warmer coat."

"Tomorrow we will go shopping. But tonight, eat your pie." Jack grinned as he scooped up the glazed cinnamon apples with a spoon.

Sara took a bite of the pie while studying the pumpkin, trying to decide whether to draw or carve a face on it. Despite being tired, she'd caught a second wind from being outdoors. She kept wondering what it was she had seen floating in the water. *What the heck is in the lake?* She wasn't sure if she should mention her concern to Jack.

"Jack, do you have a black magic marker?"

"Black magic what?" he questioned.

"A permanent marker, you know…a black felt-tip pen."

"Check in the study, below the bookshelf, inside the cabinet, left-hand side."

The chair scraped along the floor as Sara got up from the table and headed to the study. She knelt in front of the lower left cabinet and opened the door.

Two metal organizer trays sat on the top shelf of the double-shelved cabinet. Inside the trays were pens, pencils, elastic bands, and paper clips all mixed in together. Pulling them out, she separated the items and found a black Sharpie marker. After a few minutes, pens and pencils shared one tray, and paper clips and elastics neatly shared the other. *Much better.*

Returning the trays to their rightful place, she was about to close the door when she discovered a stack of coloring books on the bottom shelf. Pulling them out, she started to leaf through them. Brand new, never used, never colored-in coloring books. She didn't know what to think and now wasn't the time to ponder the books. She heard footsteps coming toward the study.

Quickly putting the coloring books back on the shelf, she closed the cabinet door and hurried to the dining area. She passed Jack as he was entering the living room.

With black marker in hand, she sat at the table in front of the pumpkin.

"What kind of face would you like Mr. Pumpkin?" she asked, speaking the words out loud. "A scary face or a happy face?"

After contemplating, she drew two big triangles for the eyes and a small triangle for the nose. Pausing for a moment, she drew a wide, half crescent-shaped mouth. She then added a few square, irregularly shaped teeth. She had finished. A simple, yet traditional-looking pumpkin face stared back at her.

She had planned to show Jack the pumpkin until she heard him yelling at the TV. Loud voices, people shouting and cheering spilled out from the living room. He was watching another football game, and she didn't want to disturb him. Instead, she picked up the pumpkin and carried it to the foyer.

Opening the front door, she stepped outside. The aspen trees quivered in the wind. Their fallen leaves had formed a natural golden carpet along the entry. They crunched, rustled, and swirled around her while she figured out where to place the pumpkin. Bending down, she decided to set it to the right of the door. Taking one last look at its face, she smiled. *Goodnight, Mr. Pumpkin.*

Sara stood up and went back inside. From the corner of his eye, Jack saw her walk by as she headed toward the dining area. While she washed the dishes and tidied up the kitchen, Jack rose from his chair and strode to the front door, realizing he had forgotten to lock it. Removing a key from his pocket, he locked the deadbolt and returned to the living room.

When Sara put the pies in the fridge, the flowers Jack had bought her were lying on the bottom shelf. Searching the cabinets, she found a glass vase and filled it with water.

Removing the cellophane from the bouquet, she arranged the flowers in the vase: sunflowers, carnations, and lilies.

Holding onto the vase, she walked out of the kitchen, past the living room, and ascended the staircase. As she strolled down the darkened hallway, a draft of cold air circled her. When she entered her bedroom, she placed the vase on the nightstand and sat down on the bed.

While admiring the flowers, she gazed over at the owl figurine for a few moments. She picked it up, inspecting it carefully. It was made of stone resin. Three small owls perched on a branch were each in a different pose. The first owl's wings covered its eyes, the second owl's wings covered its ears, and the third owl's wings covered its mouth. Inscribed on the branch below were the words: 'See no evil, hear no evil, speak no evil.' With a ghost of a smile on her lips, she placed the figurine back on the nightstand.

After changing into her pajamas, she reached for her cell phone, set the alarm and turned off the lights.

Crawling into bed, she gathered up the covers, leaned back and closed her eyes. Her thoughts drifted, recalling her mother's voice on the phone. *"Be safe, wherever you are."* She didn't have the chance to tell her mom about the tournament. She only told her she was busy, not sleeping well and losing track of time. She hadn't told anyone of her location. No one knew.

If anything happens to me, no one will ever find me.

Panic quickly took over, spinning her mind in a thousand

different directions. *What was floating in the lake? Could it have been a body?* Sitting up to catch her breath, she gripped the quilt tightly against her chest.

A floorboard creaked and her body tensed. *What was that?* Trembling with fear, tears streaked down her cheeks as she placed her head back on the pillow.

Minutes ticked by as Jack stood in the cold, dark hallway, waiting for Sara to fall asleep. Behind the bedroom door he could hear sobbing and sniffling. Then after a while…silence.

Taking a step forward, he hesitated and then turned. Shuffling back down the hallway, he mumbled under his breath.

"Eeny, meeny, miny, moe, will this one stay, or will she go?"

15

"I can't believe it. I can't even fathom it."

"What are you so riled up about?"

"You let her go out by the lake."

"Calm down, or else you will hyperventilate."

"You, of all people, I just can't believe you let her go alone."

"I was not aware that she was going. She fooled me."

"But you are not easily fooled."

"She said she was going outside to retrieve that ridiculous pumpkin of hers. I forgot I had left it under the picnic table the night before."

"So she tricked you."

"No, I was cutting a piece of pie and when I looked up, she was gone."

"That dang sweet tooth of yours is causing you trouble.

It's a constant distraction. All that sugar can't be good for you."

"Stop the lecturing."

"Did she see anything?"

"Where?"

"In the lake."

"I do not think so. She was not there very long. I went out after her and called her back inside."

"And then what happened?"

"We ate our dessert together."

"That's it?"

"Then she painted a face on the pumpkin and I watched TV. She went upstairs soon after."

"Let me repeat this one more time. You know she shouldn't be going anywhere near that lake."

"I realize that. Please quiet down."

"You shouldn't have taken her out on the boat ride. Now she's all curious."

"I already said she does not know."

"How do you know she doesn't know?"

"I have not told her anything."

"She'll find out, soon enough."

16

Sara was standing in the kitchen buttering her toast when a somber melody of bells chimed, echoing through the house.

"Sara, can you please answer the door?" Jack called out from the study.

Dropping the knife, she hurried to the foyer and opened the front door. A tall, red-haired, bearded man in a green plaid jacket stood in the doorway. He was holding a clipboard.

"Hi, I'm Ted with Connor's Custom Lighting." He smiled.

"Hi, I'm Sara, please come in, I'll— "

"Hello, sir, please follow me," Jack appeared behind Sara, motioning for Ted to follow him as he walked toward the back door.

Sara caught Ted's eye and smiled. She trailed behind them until Jack half turned to her.

"Oh Sara, could you please make us a fresh pot of coffee?" He opened the door and stepped outside with Ted.

Walking into the kitchen, she huffed under her breath and went over to the sink. Peering out the window, she watched them on the deck, trying to read their lips to decipher their words. Jack was rambling on, pointing up and along the railings on the deck. Ted kept nodding as he wrote on his clipboard.

Sara soon strolled outside holding a tray of coffee-filled cups and placed it on the picnic table. She glanced over at Ted who was taking measurements and notes. Jack stood behind him with his arms folded, darting his eyes back and forth, keeping a close watch on Ted and Sara.

"When can we have them installed?" Jack asked, shifting from one foot to the other.

"To confirm, you're going with recessed lighting for the railings and stairs plus a dual motion sensor above the door," Ted replied. He looked at Jack and then tapped on his phone. "I can do the installation on Thursday morning at nine. Will that day work for you?"

"Thursday at nine it is," Jack said, gazing at Sara. "Sara, jot that down on the calendar, will you?"

Jack shook Ted's hand and escorted him to the front door while Sara returned the coffee cups and tray to the kitchen. She picked up the cold piece of toast and pecked at it. Jack sneaked up behind her.

"My dear, what do you say we take a break and go shopping for your coat?" Winking at her, he grinned.

"Sure, it'll be nice to go out and get some fresh air."

"Well, grab your purse or whatever it is you need and we shall go."

Sara rushed up the stairs for her tote bag, flew back down and ran out the door. It had only been a few days since she arrived, but she felt suffocated. She couldn't understand how such a large place could feel so claustrophobic. She was eager to get away from the strange energy she sensed lurking inside the house.

Jack was waiting in the Cadillac with the engine idling. As she climbed into the passenger seat, she gazed over and saw him tucking his handgun into his jacket pocket. The doors clicked.

Glancing over at Sara, he put the car in reverse. "We are locked and loaded," he said. A sly smile crossed his face.

With uncertain eyes, she peered out the window as they headed down the driveway. Trying to remain calm, she took in long, deep breaths as her heart thundered in her ears.

The mid-morning sun poured through the trees, casting their shadows across the road. As the wind swayed their branches, it gave the illusion of dark figures, staggering and looming around the car.

"So tell me," tapping his thumbs on the wheel, "how is your mother?"

Lowering her chin, Sara replayed his question in her head.

"My mom…she's good," she thought for a moment, "but I don't remember talking to you about her."

"You told me about her last night."

"I did?" Squinting her eyes, she tried to remember their conversation.

"Well, perhaps you forgot. You were quite upset and went down to the lake for a while. After we had eaten our dessert, you seemed distracted. Then you decorated that pumpkin of yours."

Her throat tightened. He had rattled off her every move. *"You went down to the lake."* Her mind wandered. *I still need to find out what was floating in the water.* She remained silent, deep in thought, staring out the window.

"Sara, sometimes our mind plays tricks on us. Other times, we play tricks on our mind."

Stretching out his arm, he pressed a button on the stereo and hummed along to the music.

———————

The Cadillac pulled into the parking lot of the Fall Creek Shoppes. Sara tried to get her bearings and made a mental note of her surroundings. The outdoor shopping area featured small stores and cafés. Only a few people roamed about toting shopping bags. Jack stayed uncomfortably close to Sara as they strolled along the sidewalk.

"If my memory serves me, there is a women's clothing

store up here to the right. I suppose one would call it trendy or stylish or whatever the buzz word they are using these days."

As he pointed ahead, his arm grazed her shoulder. Immediately her thoughts went to the handgun in his pocket. She felt her leg muscles tighten and the overwhelming urge to run as fast as she could.

I need to get away from him, now.

In a state of confusion, images flashed across her mind... her clothes, her personal items. She couldn't leave them behind. All her belongings were at his house.

And then there was the upcoming tournament. The chance to win twenty-one thousand dollars. She desperately needed money to pay her bills and thought she had a good chance at winning.

Maybe her mind *was* playing tricks on her. *He wouldn't hurt me. Would he?*

"Here it is, La Rosa Boutique," Jack strutted into the store as if he owned the place.

"Good day," he waved to the two middle-aged women standing behind the counter. "This lovely lady needs a new coat," he announced.

Smiling, he turned to Sara who trudged behind him. Her face reddened as she averted their stares. One of the women, a platinum blonde, sauntered over to them. She was decked out in tight-fitting, rhinestone-trimmed jeans, a fuchsia blouse, and high-heeled boots. Sara took one look at the woman and felt frumpy in her pilled sweater, faded jeans, and scuffed ballet flats.

"Welcome to La Rosa, I'm Claudia. I can show you the items we have, please follow me."

Jack took a seat on the velvet sofa and watched as Sara followed the saleslady to the back of the store.

"You're a size eight, right?" Claudia guessed, eyeing Sara up and down.

"Yes, size medium."

Sara focused on Claudia's long magenta fingernails as they raked over the coats while she flipped through the rack. Gazing down at her own nails, unpolished and half-bitten, she couldn't remember the last time she'd had a professional manicure.

"Do you have a color preference?" Claudia asked.

"Something neutral, please."

Sara was less than enthusiastic to be there. She didn't care for malls, let alone strangers selecting her clothes. She much preferred to shop online from the comfort of home.

Claudia pulled out a three-quarter length powder blue wool coat.

"You know, with your skin tone and hair color, this one would look absolutely gorgeous on you. Here, try it on," Claudia held the coat open for her.

Sara hesitated and then slipped her arms through the sleeves. She moved toward the mirror. She saw herself swathed in a coat that tied at the waist and had wide lapels and a detachable faux fur collar. Sara spun around, tugging at the belt, and looked in the mirror again. She sighed. *Looks like something a twelve-year-old would wear.*

Jack whistled from across the store, arose from his seat, and went over to her.

"Now that is the one." His eyes widened, and his face lit up. "You must have it."

"But, it's not really my style," she said, twisting her lips into a pout. "It's not a color I typically wear."

Claudia remained silent. She glanced at Sara and then looked over at Jack.

"We will take it," Jack pulled out a wad of cash.

Sara took off the coat and handed it to Claudia who sashayed to the register. The other woman standing behind the counter leaned toward Claudia and whispered under her breath.

"Where did he find this one?" Diverting her eyes, the woman gave Sara a sidelong glance.

"That will be two hundred and sixty dollars, please," Claudia said, batting her eyelashes.

Peeling off three hundred dollar bills he slapped them on the counter.

"Keep the change ladies, lunch is on me today," Jack winked at the women.

Claudia handed Sara the coat, now on a hanger and covered in pink plastic wrap. Sara thanked her and walked out the door with her head hung low and the coat draped over her arm. Jack followed behind and caught up with her.

"What do you say, my dear, care for some lunch while we are out and about? There is a little Italian place around the corner."

"Sure, why not," she said, keeping her gaze glued to the ground. Anything was better than returning to the gloomy house.

They entered Derillo's Italian restaurant and sat at a small table by the window. It was a cozy little eatery, with its red-and-white checkered table cloths. The special of the day was fettuccine Alfredo and Jack placed two orders.

Sara sat silently, glancing around at the customers. She was curious to see if any of them looked over at Jack. Because he was a regular at the breakfast diner, she thought maybe he frequented the same places. But no one seemed to acknowledge him, and the waitress didn't appear to recognize him when she took the order.

Jack twirled the creamy noodles around his fork, about to take a mouthful, when his cell phone rang. He pulled it from his pocket, stood up from the table, and stepped outside to take the call.

Sara chowed down on her pasta and looked out the window. She watched as he paced back and forth with the phone pressed to his ear. She continued to observe him as he toyed with his phone. He would make a call, check on Sara through the window, end the call, and gaze back at her. He repeated the sequence numerous times. Fifteen minutes had elapsed.

Sara waited patiently with her elbows on the table, her chin resting in her palms. When Jack walked back inside, he stopped to chat with the waitress before heading to the table.

"Are you ready to go?" He tossed two twenties on the table.

Sliding her chair back, Sara stood up and reached for her tote bag while the waitress handed Jack a small takeout container. They walked out of the restaurant.

Back in the car, they headed for Shady Bend Road. Out of town and into the woods they traveled. Over the past few days, Sara had become aware of Jack's ever-changing moods. He went from happy to sad at a moment's notice.

As he hummed along to the music, he appeared to be content. She figured it was a good enough time to ask him a question she had been holding in the back of her mind.

"Jack, may I ask you something?"

"Yes, what is it?" Reaching over, he turned the volume down on the stereo.

"I don't mean to pry, but I was wondering…what do you do?"

"What do I do? Why, I do whatever it takes." He grinned.

She gave him a sideways glance.

"No, I meant for a living. What do you do for a living?"

"Hmm…what do I do for a living?" Clicking his tongue, he glanced over at her. "Well, one could say that I profit from my ability to outthink my opponents." Curling his lips, a wry smile lingered on his face.

Sara remained quiet, pondering his answer. *That line sounds familiar. He said something about 'opponents' when we first met. 'Rules of the game and know thy opponent.'*

Hesitant, she turned to him. "Does that mean you play games for a living?"

"One could say that."

"Poker? Is it the tournaments? Do you play cards for real money?"

"Ooh, smart girl. Now you are getting warmer," he teased.

"So, you're a professional gambler then."

"Everything is a gamble; life is nothing but a game." The corners of his mouth twitched. "All you have to do is know how to play."

Fixing his eyes on the road, he stared dead ahead.

Sara climbed the stairs with her new coat hanging over her shoulder. Upon entering her room, she opened the wardrobe and hung it on the rod. She soon heard the sound of footsteps tromping down the hall toward her bedroom. Jack appeared in the doorway.

"Sara, sorry to bother you but when you have a minute, I put a piece of paper with a list of appointments on my desk. Would you be so kind as to record them on the computer or your phone, to help remind me of them?"

"Okay, I'll be down shortly. Oh, and Jack, thank you for the coat."

"My pleasure, I cannot wait to see it on you again," he said, wiggling his eyebrows.

She forced a smile.

"What is it, my dear? You seem to be troubled."

"It's nothing, really."

"Sara, come now, I can tell."

She glanced down at the floor for a few seconds and then looked up at him.

"I could have bought my own coat, you know."

"I realize that. Perhaps I thought most young women like to receive gifts every now and then."

"I appreciate the thought, but it just felt a little weird to me. I prefer to buy my own clothing."

"Well, if you do not like it, you can always return it."

"No, it's okay." She half smiled.

"Why do I sense something else is going on here?"

She looked away, uncertain if she should ask him...or tell him what was really on her mind. She was afraid of upsetting him.

"Sara, please, what is it?"

She sucked in a breath and let it out. "The other day, at the diner, when you were telling me about the girl who helped with the last tournament..."

"Sheila?"

"Yeah."

"What about her?"

"Did she ever go out on the lake...on boat rides with you?"

"Why do you ask?" he narrowed his eyes.

"Oh, nothing really...I was just curious, I guess." A nervous smile crept across her face.

An uncomfortable moment of silence fell between them.

"Are there any other questions you would like answered?" Staring at her he held her gaze, "Ask now, or forever hold your peace."

"No," she quickly shook her head.

"Well, then, for the record, Sheila did not go out on the boat or anywhere near the lake. She was deathly afraid of the water. She did not know how to swim."

Sara was at a loss for words.

"On a side note, young lady, I suggest you work on your poker face because your emotions are written all over it."

"I know. Others have told me I'm not very good at hiding them," her voice dipped as she lowered her head.

"You wear them well." Taking a step forward, he leaned into her. "However, in certain circumstances, it may not serve you."

"How do you mean?"

"Well, for instance, you are the kind of gal, who, as they say, lays all her cards on the table. You appear to be sincere with all that you say and do. But sometimes, one must play her cards close to her chest."

"What does that mean?"

"In the game of poker, it means you do not allow other players to see the cards you hold. In the game of life, as I mentioned earlier, it means you need to be a bit more cautious with people...shall I say, a bit more covert." Winking at her, he turned away and headed back down the hallway.

Sara drew in a deep breath and slowly let it out, thinking about their conversation. She wondered if there was a hidden message in Jack's words. What was it exactly that he was trying to convey? Moments later, she heard the sound of his bedroom door close.

Descending the stairs, Sara went into the study. While scanning Jack's paper-strewn desk, she observed the cordless phone sitting on its base. The screen glowed bright orange. *He must have put new batteries in it.* The call counter flashed the number 19. *What's going on with this phone? Nineteen missed calls or messages? Can that be right?*

Locating the piece of paper with the scribbled list, she picked it up and walked over to her desk. She opened the laptop and placed the paper beside it, reading the words out loud as she typed.

After logging the appointments into the computer, she entered them on her cell phone calendar when the clock chimed, interrupting her. She looked up at the wall and watched the little red bird rock back and forth and cuckoo six times.

As she turned back to the computer, she caught sight of the moose head. Its black, glassy eyes moved slightly and looked directly at her. She did a double take.

Rising from the chair, she walked over and stood in front of the moose. With her eyes intensely focused on the animal head, she watched and waited a few moments, but the moose's eyes didn't move. She shook her head and then massaged her forehead. *I must be imagining things.*

Sara was exhausted. Since arriving at Jack's house, she'd slept maybe seven hours total in three days. Longing for a good night's sleep, she trudged up the stairs and plodded down the cold, drafty hallway.

Once in her bedroom, she closed the curtains and collapsed on the bed. She was too tired to change her clothes and put on pajamas. She stared at the ceiling, squinting her eyes as the middle bulb on the overhead track light beamed down on her. When she reached over to the switch to turn off the lights, she froze.

On the nightstand, next to the three owls, written in sunflower petals was the word 'stay.'

She shot up straight to catch her breath and slowly gazed around the room, not blinking, not knowing what she was looking for. She began to quiver, uncertain if from fear or the frigid air that swirled in the room.

18

"What's this, leftovers?"

"Fettuccini Alfredo, I hardly touched it."

"Where did you get it?"

"It is from that little Italian restaurant, you know, the one at the outdoor mall."

"You went shopping today? What did you buy?"

"I bought her a new coat."

"That was thoughtful of you."

"Yes, well, I do not think she likes it."

"What makes you say that?"

"Never mind."

"What's wrong? Something's wrong."

"She was asking about Sheila again."

"And?"

"She asked me if Sheila went out on the lake. If she went on boat rides."

"What did you say?"

"I told her she did not…"

"Ooh, this pasta is delicious. I haven't eaten all day."

"Slow down, you eat too fast."

"So, I have something to share."

"What?"

"I have a little confession."

"Oh?"

"I did something."

"What did you do?"

"It wasn't that bad."

"Well, what did you do?"

"I may have frightened her."

"Now why would you go and do that?"

"Because you haven't introduced us yet. You can't keep me in the dark forever."

"I will keep you here as long as I see fit. Now for the last time, what did you do?"

"I sent her a message."

"A message? How did you send it?"

"I sneaked in her room and left it on the nightstand."

"You went into her room? Did she see you?"

"No, I went into the room when she was downstairs in the study."

"What did the message say?"

"It was just a single word."

"What did it say?"

"Stay."

19

At 5:00 the next morning, Jack walked into the study and found Sara sitting at her desk. Smiling, he strolled over to her.

"Well, well, well, what do we have here…an early bird catching the worm?"

She didn't reply.

"Sara," he said, raising his voice.

She gazed up at him. Dark circles shadowed her eyes. Her face was sallow, and her hair was tied in a messy knot on top of her head. She was wrapped in her new powder blue coat and had the fur collar covering her ears.

"Is something wrong?" he placed his hand on her shoulder. "You do not look well."

"I'm f-f-freezing," she stammered, teeth chattering.

"Come now," he said, offering his arm, "I will light a fire."

Grabbing hold of his forearm, Sara lifted herself out of the chair, legs weak and wobbling beneath her. He guided her into the living room and over to the fireplace.

A large copper bucket filled with firewood sat on the floor. He picked up a log, placed it on the grate and reached for an old newspaper on the end table. Tearing off a few sheets, he crumpled them up and placed them under the log. After striking a match, he lit the papers and stepped back to position the mesh iron screen in front of the fireplace.

As the log caught fire, orange flames curled, rising and flickering. The pine wood crackled. Sara stood hypnotized, swaying, as she held her hands out toward the heat. Jack dragged a chair over to the fireplace.

"Here," he motioned to her, "sit down and warm up."

Turning around, she plopped into the chair and sank into the cushion. "Thank you," she whispered.

"How about I make you some breakfast?"

She gave him a slow nod and Jack darted out of the living room.

Her eyes drifted up and along the fireplace to a set of picture frames atop the mantel. They were empty. *I don't remember seeing those before.* As she gazed at each frame, blurry, distorted photos started to appear. Leaning in closer, she blinked several times and looked again. The photos faded away.

As she rested her head on the chair back, her breathing grew shallow. The warmth of the fire washed over her, thawing her chilled body. She fought to keep her eyes open, but the weight of her eyelids helped them to close.

———

Clang, Clang, Clang.

Startled awake by a loud noise, Sara was disoriented. She rubbed her eyes and looked down and saw a red plaid blanket draped over her legs and feet. Gripping the arms of the chair, she eased herself upright. The blanket fell to the floor.

As she reached down to retrieve it, she saw his black rubber-soled shoes. She slowly looked up. Jack was standing over her, holding a small iron shovel.

"Welcome back," he said. "You went out like a light." He leaned the shovel up against the fireplace and held his hand in front of her. "Stay put. I will bring you your breakfast."

Ten minutes later, he returned to the living room with a small bowl of oatmeal and a cup of tea. Sara stood up to turn the chair around when Jack set the tray on the table.

"Thank you," she said, brushing her hair from her eyes. "Sorry I fell asleep."

"There is nothing to be sorry about; you needed your rest. Are you feeling better?"

"A little bit." She took a sip of tea. It was scalding hot and burned the back of her throat. "What time is it?"

"It is eight thirty." Walking over to the fireplace, he picked up the shovel and began swinging it by his side. "I will need to leave by nine for my appointment. If you are too tired, you can stay here."

"No, I'll be fine. I just need to freshen up."

Jack bent down to scoop up the ashes and cover the embers. Sara finished her breakfast and then lumbered up the stairs.

After a warm shower and change of clothes, she headed back down the hallway. From a distance, she could see Jack's bedroom door was ajar. As she drew near, she saw him walk toward the doorway and could hear him muttering under his breath. *He must be on his cell phone.* Slowing her gait, she padded softly. When she reached the landing, the door slammed shut. Jack staggered toward her.

"Are you ready to go, my dear?"

Half smiling, Sara grabbed hold of the banister and made her way down the stairs. She followed him through the kitchen to another door beyond the pantry and peered past his shoulder as he unlocked and opened it. They entered the garage, Jack walking over to the black Cadillac Escalade occupying the middle bay. He stepped up onto the running board and hoisted himself into the seat.

On one side of the garage, storage shelves lined the length of the wall. Sara gazed up at the top shelf and saw an assortment of luggage. Her gaze soon turned into a stare. The suitcases were a mix of different colors and sizes, some hard sided, while others were soft. A confused expression crossed her face.

"Sara, come now, time to climb upon my trusty steed," he called out from the driver's side window. Pressing the remote attached to the visor, the garage door vibrated as it inched its way up.

She turned around and walked toward the vehicle, sidestepping a stockpile of water jugs on the stained concrete floor. Opening the door, she climbed in.

"Did you just call your truck a trusty steed?"

"Yes, it is my work horse. Would you have preferred that I call it my black stallion?"

"Truck, horse, stallion…it's your call."

"It is not a truck; it is an SUV, a luxury SUV, for your information."

"Whatever you say."

Jack backed the Escalade out of the garage, past his car parked in the driveway. Gravel flew from under the tires as he spun around, stopping alongside the sedan. He reached into his pocket, pulled out the key fob for the Cadillac and tossed it in Sara's lap.

"Climb into that car and follow me," he ordered.

Cocking her head, she picked up the key fob, studying it. "But I…"

"But what? You told me you needed a car to drive while you are here. Did you not?"

"What I meant was…"

"Well, what you meant does not matter right now. What I need is for you to follow me, to my appointment. The

Escalade is being fitted with winter tires and the Caddy needs its brakes checked." He glowered at her.

Sara stepped out of the SUV and walked to the sedan.

Jack leaned out of the window, "You will need to keep that key in your pocket or in the car. It is a remote transmitter. The car will not start without it."

"Okay," she said, slipping the key into her coat pocket. She reached for the handle and opened the door.

Jack watched while she sat behind the wheel, adjusting the mirrors and fumbling with the push-button to start the engine. As she strapped the seat belt across her chest, she glanced over at him. He nodded and gave her a thumbs up. With both hands clamped on the steering wheel, she followed the Escalade as it rolled down the long driveway and turned right.

Distracted by images of suitcases flitting through her mind, she lagged behind Jack as they traveled down the deserted road.

What the heck is he doing with all that mismatched luggage? Do they belong to the other girls? On the boat ride, he said there were others. Did they disappear too? Like Sheila? Something's not right. I need to find a police station.

Upon reaching the main roadway, Sara slowed the car as she approached the intersection. She could feel the way the brakes had a soft, spongy feel to them under her foot.

But if I go to the police, he'll just follow me there. Besides, he might know them all...it's a small town. Who will they

believe, me or him? He'll probably just tell them the luggage
belongs to him anyhow.

When the traffic light turned red, she leaned over to the
passenger seat and stuck her arm inside her tote bag, digging
for her cell phone. The bristles on her hairbrush scraped the
back of her hand as she felt past her wallet, makeup compact,
and keys. *Please, please be in here.*

She turned her tote upside down and gave it a good shake,
its contents spilling onto the seat and floor. She quickly
glanced at her stuff. Her cell phone wasn't there.

"Oh no! I don't have my phone," she shouted, banging her
fist on the steering wheel.

Jack stared at her through his rearview mirror, smiling as
she fidgeted. The light changed to green. Her fleeting thought
of driving off in search of a police station was soon forgotten.

They traveled along the main road for a few miles, and
when they passed Redfield's Market, Jack turned onto a side
street. Ahead, to the left, stood a gray brick building with four
garage doors. The sign out front read TIERNEY AUTOMOTIVE.
Jack pulled into the lot, hopped out of his Escalade, and
headed inside the building.

Sara entered the lot and quickly parked the car. While
gathering up her things on the seat and stuffing them back into
her tote, she looked around again for her cell phone. She slid
her hand between the console and passenger seat as far down
as she could. *Nothing.*

Unbuckling the seat belt, she leaned over, put her hand

under the seat, and patted the floorboard. Something cold, hard, and cylindrical met her fingers. With caution, she pulled out a small flashlight.

Jack rapped his knuckles on the driver's side window. Her body jerked at the sudden sound. Hesitating, she remained slouched over, holding the flashlight as she turned her head toward him.

"What are you doing in there?" He glared at her with eyes wide, and lips parted.

Pushing herself upright, she looped her arm through the straps of her tote, the flashlight slipping from her hand and into the bag. She exited the car and followed him inside. With her tote bag secured over her shoulder and held tight against her side, she walked over near the water cooler and took a seat. Jack, sporting a wide grin, sat down next to her.

"What time is my doctor's appointment?" he asked, tapping his foot and checking his watch.

"I'm not sure, I forgot my phone." Gazing up at him, she frowned.

"Forgot your phone? Why I thought that thing was attached to you by some invisible cord. You are never without it." Staring her down, he waited for a reply.

Sara looked away. Her eyes glazed over and grew distant. Her thoughts wandered back to the house, back to the garage, back to the luggage on top of the shelf.

What the hell is he doing with a pink polka dot suitcase?

20

The carpet pattern made Sara dizzy as she followed Jack down the long hallway. With each step she took, multi-colored abstract circles spiraled beneath her feet as she trailed her fingers along the wall to steady herself.

Jack stopped in front of a door with the number nine written on it. The nameplate read Dr. Walter Moss, MD. Turning the metal handle, he motioned for Sara to enter.

They stepped into a brightly lit waiting room lined with blue chairs. An older woman with a beehive hairdo sat behind a small sliding-glass window. Dressed in a floral print blouse, she wore thick, dark-rimmed glasses. She looked up at them when she heard the door close.

"Do you have an appointment?" the woman asked, fixing her eyes on Sara.

"Me?" Sara pointed to herself, "No."

"Well, you do look a tad pale, my dear," Jack piped in as he brushed past her to the window.

"Jack Halvrek here for Dr. Moss," he said to the woman, flashing a toothy grin.

Sara spotted a bunch of old magazines on a table, picked one up, and settled into a chair near the door. Thumbing through the pages she glanced around for a restroom, tiny beads of sweat dotting her hairline as her stomach flooded with waves of nausea. The woman behind the desk glanced over at Sara and saw her leaning forward in the chair, arms wrapped around her abdomen.

"Are you okay, Miss?" the woman asked, a hint of concern in her voice.

"I'm not feeling well. May I use your restroom, please?" Sara asked.

"Yes, out the door and to your right."

Rising from the chair with a hand on her stomach, Sara barreled out the door. She held her head high to avoid the swirling carpet as she raced on unsteady legs to the bathroom. She threw open the bathroom door and rushed to the sink.

Gazing into the mirror, she gripped the edge of the countertop. Sunken eyes stared back at her from a pasty white complexion.

She turned on the faucet and cupped her hands under the spout. As cold water streamed into her palms, she drank handfuls, quenching her thirst. Minutes passed as she lingered over the sink, splashing water on her face.

Banging his fist on the bathroom door, Jack called out to her. "My dear, are you in there? Is everything okay?"

"I need a few more minutes," she groaned.

Jack leaned back against the wall and started humming a little tune while he waited for her to exit the restroom.

Five minutes later, the door opened, and Sara stumbled out of the bathroom. Jack moved toward her, placing the back of his hand on her forehead.

"You are not well," he said. "We need to get you home."

"I must have a stomach bug or something," turning her head, she stepped away from him.

"You are in no shape to drive. We will leave my car here and pick it up another day."

"No, no, you don't have to do that, I'll be okay. I just need some fresh air." Increasing her pace, she focused on the exit door at the end of the hallway.

Once outside the building, Sara made a beeline to the Cadillac. Jack trailed behind as he neared the Escalade parked a few spots away. She could feel his eyes on her studying her every move, but she refused to glance back or pay attention to him.

Jack climbed into his vehicle, started the engine, and pulled out of the parking lot. Eyeing his Cadillac through the rearview mirror, he kept a watchful gaze as Sara followed him. They traveled back along the main road, taking a right and heading toward the lake.

Powering down the window, Sara inhaled long, deep breaths

of the brisk air. "Breathe, just breathe," she repeated out loud. The window remained open during her drive back to the house.

Dragging her feet up the stairs and down the hallway, Sara entered her bedroom. She flung her coat over the chair and kicked off her shoes. Clutching her stomach with both hands, she collapsed on the bed.

She yanked at the quilt to cover her shivering body and rested her head on the pillow. *I'm tired and now sick. I just want to go home to my apartment, my bed. I need sleep.*

Rolling over on her side, she curled up into a tight ball and closed her eyes. Darkness fell as she drifted into dreamland...

The last rays of the sun shone on the lake turning the waters indigo blue. From the place where she lay, a gentle wave churned below. The cold, hard surface rocked back and forth, swaying her from side to side.

Opening her eyes, she blinked to the clouded sky above. She lifted her head and sat up slowly, steadying herself. Queasiness surged inside her stomach.

A voice from below the darkened lake called to her, "Sara, Sara."

Peering over the side of the small wooden boat, she leaned in for a closer look. She gasped as a hand rose from the misty waters, reached up, and grabbed hold of her arm.

Screaming, she fought to break free as the hand tightened its grip.

"Sara, Sara," the voice spoke louder.

Her body shook as she struggled to breathe…

Sara opened her eyes to find Jack hovering over her, his hand resting on her forearm.

"You look like an angel when you sleep," he whispered.

Groggy and confused, she propped herself up on her elbows while Jack remained next to the bed, leering at her.

"I came to check on you. You were sleeping so peacefully." A faint smile raised the corners of his mouth.

"How long have you been here?" she asked, her voice strained. Pushing herself upright to a sitting position, she pulled the covers closer.

"Not too long, I brought you some tea. As I was leaving, you began to whimper and thrash about. I figured you had had a bad dream."

He sat down on the edge of the bed and stared into her eyes. "I was thinking how nice it would be if you could stay here…in our own little world. Our safe, secure, quiet little world. We have each other, what more do we need?"

Looking away, without expression, Sara let her gaze wander over to the window.

"Are you okay, my dear? How are you feeling?"

"I feel as if I need to go home. I'm not sure if—"

"Home? You have just arrived, you cannot leave now."

He shot up from the bed and started pacing the room. "Is something wrong? Is there something you are not telling me?"

"No, it's just that I haven't been sleeping much, and now I'm not feeling well," she couldn't hide the emotion in her voice.

"Sara, did you forget you offered to help me? A deal is a deal." He held his mouth in a tight line.

"I'm exhausted. Maybe one of the other players can take my place and help out. I think it's best if I go home."

"That may not be an option. I have been watching the news. A winter storm is on the horizon, and they are forecasting snow as early as Saturday morning. Road restrictions will be in place." His face relaxed into a smile.

Turning on his heel, he walked out of the room closing the door behind him.

Sara looked over at the cup of tea on the nightstand. Next to it, on top of an envelope, was a small white box tied with a pink ribbon. Picking up the box, she held it to her ear and gave it a quick shake, then placed it on her lap. She tore open the envelope and pulled out the paper inside, unfolding it carefully.

Dear Sara,

Please accept this small token of my appreciation. Because you were not too thrilled with the coat, perhaps this gift is more suitable. I do hope you like it.

Regards, Jack

Placing the letter aside, she untied the ribbon and opened the box. A delicate silver chain sat atop a tiny square of white cotton. Taking it out of the box, she held it up in front of her, a bracelet with a silver charm. She fingered the dangling charm, the letter 'S.' She wasn't quite sure what to make of it.

21

"Keep your voice down. She might hear you."

"And if she does?"

"She does not know you are here."

"You still haven't told her?"

"No."

"So, do you plan on telling her before the weekend?"

"I have no idea."

"What do you mean you have no idea?"

"I said I have no idea, now enough."

"Okay, but."

"But what?"

"You've been gone all day."

"I had appointments in town. I was busy."

"Did she accompany you?"

"Yes."

"I thought you were going to introduce us today."

"No, not today, it was not the right time. She is not feeling well."

"Is she sick?"

"Yes, I found her sitting in the study early this morning. She looked terrible. I felt bad dragging her along, but she insisted."

"Did you see Walter today?"

"Yes."

"And what did the good doctor have to say?"

"Nothing new but the same old, same old."

"Did she meet him?"

"No, she ran off to the bathroom. I said she is not feeling well."

"Is that the reason you went into her room after you arrived home?"

"Yes, I brought her some tea and a little gift. I was hoping it would make her feel better."

"A gift?"

"Yes."

"What kind of gift?"

"A bracelet."

"Let me guess, is it silver?"

"Yes, why?"

"And it has her initial?"

"Yes, is there a problem?"

"Does she like it?"

"I do not know yet."

"I can't wait to hear what she says."

Sara stood at the top of the stairway listening to the muffled voices below, unable to determine what they were saying. As she inched her way down the stairs, she lost her balance halfway and latched onto the banister. Quickly composing herself, she continued down the stairs.

Jack shot a quick glance over his shoulder and caught her eye.

"So glad you could join us this morning," he said, clapping his hands as she stepped into the foyer. He introduced Sara to the burly, raven-haired man standing next to him.

"Sara, this is Adam. He will install our outdoor lights today."

Bewildered, she looked at Jack and then at Adam. He was

wearing a flannel shirt and jeans. She glanced at the tool belt strapped around his waist.

"Oh, you must work with Ted, right? At Connor's Custom Lighting." In her peripheral vision, she saw Jack shake his head at him.

"Jack was just telling me you've been sick. Hope you're feeling better," Adam said. He gave her a tight-lipped smile.

"I'm fine, thanks," she replied and then turned to face Jack. "I need to talk to you," lowering her voice, "in private."

"What is it? I am about to escort Adam to the deck."

"I forgot to ask you the other day...about the sunflower petals—"

"Sunflower petals?"

"Yes, next to the owls on the—"

"Owls? Sunflower petals?" he repeated, his eyebrows drawn together. "What are you talking about? You must be imagining things."

"No, I'm not 'imagining' things," she said, air-quoting the word.

"Well, perhaps you dreamt about them."

"No, I didn't dream about them either. The owls, on the nightstand...next to them, the sunflower petals...they spelled out a word. Then there's the moose...the one on the wall. His eyes...follow me and stare." Her eyes grew wide as she mimicked the moose.

"Now that is enough. There will be no more crazy talk," he said, waving his hand to shush her. "Adam and I have work to do, and so do you. Filing needs to be taken care of in the study." Glaring at her through vacant eyes, he spoke slowly, enunciating each word. "Please…see…to…it."

Sara looked at Adam. He stood with his thumbs hooked in his belt, staring down at his mud-caked work boots. Eyeing him, she waited a few seconds and then stomped away.

"Follow me," Jack said, as he patted Adam on the shoulder. "Do not mind her. She is a bit delirious. Poor gal has not been sleeping well for some reason."

They walked through the house toward the back door.

Upon entering the study, Sara came to a halt. Papers were strewn everywhere, littering the floor. The binders sat opened and overturned on the long table against the wall. It was a mess again.

She dropped to her knees, covering her face with both hands. *He's on my last nerve.* Releasing a long breath, she sat back on her heels and contemplated.

After a few minutes, she stood up and collected all the papers. When she stacked them on the table, she noticed some of the pages had only a word or two written on them. Leafing through the papers, she became alarmed by what she read.

Lock Up
Under the Gun
Shootout
Blind, Chop
Down the River

Her hands trembled as she held onto the papers and rushed

over to her desk. *What the hell is going on here? Is this some sort of sick game he's playing?*

Her pulse quickened as she flipped open the laptop. She thought she heard a noise. Looking around the room, she glanced over at the doorway. No one was there.

The computer powered on and she pulled up a search engine. She entered the words in the search bar. She soon discovered their link to poker terminology. *Card games.* She read through all of the definitions to be sure.

While somewhat relieved, she still felt a bit unnerved. *Is everything just a game to him? I feel like a pawn in some crazy game.*

A calendar alert popped up on the computer, '4:00 p.m. Virginia piano.' She focused on the reminder. *Who's Virginia? I wonder what that's all about...maybe the piano is broken or something.*

As she sat at the computer, staring at the screen, she began to shiver. Rubbing her hands up and down her arms, she tried to warm herself. *It's so cold in here.* It didn't feel like Jack had turned on the heat. She thought about lighting the fireplace but wasn't sure if her independent act would upset him. She didn't want to interrupt him while he was outside with Adam, so she headed up to her room to grab her coat.

At the top of the stairs, a ray of light beamed into the hallway. She looked to her right. Jack's bedroom door was slightly ajar. Walking over to the door, she pushed it open and poked her head inside, taken aback by what she saw.

Sara had envisioned his bedroom to be in shambles and was surprised by its tidiness, its spaciousness. The room was huge.

Stepping inside, she walked over to a sitting area with an oversized leather chair and ottoman. The king-sized bed with its thick wooden headboard was covered with a buffalo plaid quilt. A raggedy teddy bear sat on top of one of the pillows.

That's kind of bizarre. She giggled.

Across from the bed, a mid-sized TV monitor sat atop a dark wooden dresser. Off to the right was a bathroom and along the wall, a sliding door. Sara went over and slid the door open to a large walk-in closet. Western-style shirts in all different colors hung from the rod above, and jeans folded over hangers hung below. On the floor, clear plastic bins stacked on top of each other appeared to contain towels, blankets, and bedding.

Sliding the door closed, she turned back to the room and spotted two large cardboard boxes in the corner. She walked over to them. One box was sealed with tape, the other folded closed. A tape gun dispenser was sitting on top of it. Picking up the tape gun, she hesitated for a second and then placed it on the floor. Carefully unfolding the flaps, she opened the box and peeked inside.

What the heck? It was full of neatly folded clothes— women's clothes.

On top of the clothes sat a pair of shoes and a white

handbag. The handbag looked brand new. She took it out, set it aside, and continued rummaging through the box.

"Quack, quack, quack. Quack, quack, quack." *What's going on out there?*

She crept over to the three large windows overlooking the lake and peered into the backyard. She could see Jack standing at the bottom of the deck. He had a pair of binoculars hanging around his neck and was tossing something up and down in his hand. Lifting his arm, he threw whatever he was holding toward the dock.

Sara looked over, following his line of vision. Three ducks were running back to the water, flapping their wings. Jack bent down to the ground, picked something up, and hurled it into the air, toward the dock again.

What the…? Is he throwing rocks at those little ducks? That's cruel!

Outraged, she placed her hands on the window, about to pound on the glass, when she realized she wasn't supposed to be in the room. She was supposed to be working in the study…filing. She wasn't supposed to be by his window or snooping around. Instead, she kept her arms close to her side her hands balled into fists and continued to curse him under her breath.

She watched as he walked through the yard and stopped just before he reached the dock. He raised the binoculars and looked out at the lake, turning his head slowly as he scanned the waters. Fixing his gaze on something, he lowered the binoculars. Sara pressed her cheek to the window, trying to see the object he was looking at.

A few seconds later, Jack turned around and looked back at the house. Raising the binoculars to his eyes, he tipped his head back and looked up toward his room. Sara gasped, instantly crouching below the window.

Oh no! I hope he didn't see me.

On hands and knees, she crawled across the floor as fast as her racing pulse, too afraid to stand up.

Oh hell! The clothes. She crawled back over to the box and hunched over it.

"Sara, oh, Sara."

Whipping her head around, she heard Jack yelling for her from downstairs. Her adrenaline surged as she quickly stuffed the items back inside the box, hands trembling as she tucked the flaps together.

When she placed the tape dispenser back on top, she glanced down at the handbag still lying on the floor.

Crap!

Snatching it, she slung it over her shoulder and stood up. Quietly closing the door behind her, she dashed down the hall toward her room.

"Sara, where are you?" Jack called out again, his voice sounding closer. "I need you to come outside this minute."

"I'll be right there," she shouted.

Stuffing the handbag inside her suitcase, under her clothes, she grabbed her coat and hurried back down the hallway. She paused on the landing. She could see Jack standing in the foyer below. Inhaling a deep breath, she slowly exhaled as she took hold of the banister. Jack watched as she descended the stairs.

"I see you have finished filing in the study," he said.

"Yeah, I straightened it out," she said, clearing her throat, "everything's back in order."

"Well, this evening we should be able to put the handbooks together for the tournament. Last night, while you were resting, it took me hours to print out all the pages."

Slipping her arm into the sleeve of her coat, he noticed she was trembling.

"What else have you been doing today?" he asked, eyebrows lifted.

Pulling her coat over her shoulders, she looked toward the study. "Organizing my desk. It was so cold in the study, I thought about starting a fire…I mean lighting a fire…in the fireplace, but I didn't want to disturb you."

"Are you okay? You are shaking."

"I'm just cold, that's all."

"Well, button up and follow me." He turned and headed for the back door.

With her heart still racing, Sara followed him outside. Adam was gathering his tools and glimpsed at Sara when she stepped onto the deck. He'd just finished installing the motion sensor light above the door. Jack walked over to him, patted him on the back and handed him a fistful of cash. Five minutes later, Adam was gone.

"What do you think of our new lights?" Strolling around the deck, Jack pointed to all the new lighting along the railing.

"They look great," she replied, as she walked to the end of the deck, pretending to look at the lights on the stairs. "Can't wait to see how they look at night."

Turning her head toward the lake, she scanned the waters, searching for the ducks. Concerned for their safety, she hoped they weren't injured.

"Yes, well, I thought our guests might want to spend some time outside in the evening and enjoy the fresh, clean air." He took a step toward her. "I also thought perhaps the next time you peer out the window, you will be able to see things more clearly." Jack stood with his arms folded, waiting for her to return his gaze.

At four o'clock, the doorbell sounded. Jack swaggered to the foyer and opened the front door.

"Well, hello Ms. Mullberry," he said, a wide grin forming on his face.

"Good afternoon Mr. Halvrek," the woman replied.

"Please, come in." Leaning over, he kissed her on the cheek. "And how have you been?"

"Fine and dandy, sir, and you?"

"Quite well, thank you for asking."

Virginia Mullberry, a petite woman in her sixties, walked into the house looking as if she'd stepped out of the 1930s. Dressed in a mid-length black frock with a matching coat, she carried a vintage doctor's bag with both hands gripping the handle. Her impeccably coiffed jet black hair and her ruby stained lips were a stark contrast to her alabaster skin.

"This way, madam," Jack motioned for her to follow him.

With her nose in the air, Virginia pranced through the living room, her lace-up heeled oxfords clip-clopping across the floor. As she passed by the fireplace, she eyed the picture frames on the mantel, going over to them to take a closer look.

"And who might this be?" Standing on tiptoes, she inspected the photos.

"That would be Miss Sara," he replied.

Smiling, Virginia wriggled out of her coat and draped it over a chair. She walked over to the piano and sat down on the cushioned bench. Unzipping her bag, she removed her tools and placed them beside her. Jack pulled up a chair next to her as she began playing the piano.

As her fingers stroked the same few keys over and over, the notes formed a haunting tune. Sara worked in the study and heard the sounds of the piano echoing throughout the house.

When Virginia added a chord, the music turned darker. Spooked by the ominous tone, Sara rubbed at the goosebumps on her arms as she got up from the desk and slowly made her way to the living room. With each step she took, the music grew louder.

Jack looked up and touched Virginia's arm when he saw Sara walking toward them. The music stopped.

"Sara, my dear, there you are," he said. "Come and say hello to Virginia."

Virginia stood up from the bench, smoothing her frock. Sara thought her outfit was rather odd, and that she looked a bit peculiar. She resembled a character from an old black-and-white silent film.

"Pleased to meet you, Sara." Virginia smiled, extending her hand. "You are quite a photogenic young woman."

Puzzled by her comment, Sara gently shook Virginia's dainty hand.

"Nice to meet you, but please excuse me, I don't know what you mean by photogenic."

"The lovely photos of you on the mantel," Virginia replied.

Turning around, Sara crept over to the fireplace and gazed at the picture frames. A chill prickled her skin, and the tiny hairs on the back of her neck stood on end. Her mouth gaped open as she studied the four pictures on the mantel, all photos of her.

In the first frame, she was standing by the living room window, gazing at the lake. Judging by her outfit, it appeared to have been taken the day of her arrival. The second picture was one of her sitting at her desk in the study. She was smiling with the phone to her ear.

The third photo was a snapshot of her standing by the mirror at the clothing store wearing the powder blue coat. The fourth photo was taken at the Italian restaurant. She looked pensive as she sat at the table, staring out the window.

Sara's gaze dropped to the floor. She felt violated. She

didn't know what to think. She had no idea Jack had taken photos of her.

"My dear, is something wrong?" he asked.

"I wasn't aware of you taking my picture…these pictures," she huffed. "It's a little unsettling."

"Do not be troubled by a few photos."

"But I didn't give you permission to take them. Isn't that illegal?"

"Illegal? You are in my house, in my possession," he glared at her.

"But why did you take them?" she demanded, crossing her arms.

"In case something happens to you."

"In case something happens to me? What is that supposed to mean?" her eyes grew wide. "Are you planning on having something happen to me?"

"Now, now, here you go with the crazy talk again. If you continue, we will have to trade your pretty blue coat for a straight jacket."

Sara was speechless.

"We will discuss your concerns later. Virginia needs to finish tuning the piano. Perhaps you can bring us some tea and a plate of those ginger cookies I purchased the other day." Grinning ear to ear, he turned his attention back to Virginia.

Sara scurried from the living room, heading to the kitchen to prepare their refreshments. Twisting the faucet handle, she filled the kettle and placed it on the stove.

That's the second time today he called me crazy. Crazy talk, how dare he.

Virginia began playing the piano again, and an uneasy feeling swept over Sara as the menacing tone reverberated throughout the house.

Now they're both driving me up a wall.

She flung open the pantry door and pulled the box of cookies off the shelf. Opening the inner plastic wrap, she put a handful of cookies onto a dish. As the kettle began whistling, she lifted it from the stove and poured the boiling water into two cups. She then placed the items on the tray and marched back to the living room.

The teacups rattled against the saucers as she set the tray down on the side table. She was a bundle of nerves.

"Can I bring you anything else?" she asked, silently wishing they would stop the sinister music.

Jack stood up, examining the tray and handing Virginia a cup of tea.

"That will be all," he said, looking back at Sara. Picking up a cookie, he dipped it in his tea and shoved it in his mouth.

Sara turned around and returned to the study. The piano music stopped, and she sighed with relief. She needed to focus on the task at hand. She went over to the table and began assembling the handbooks for the tournament.

"Sara, my dear, where have you run off to now?" Jack called out as his footsteps thudded across the floor.

"Coming," she replied. She took a deep breath, and

walked out of the study. They met in the foyer and stood face to face.

"There you are. You keep disappearing on me," he said, arching an eyebrow. "Would you mind retrieving an envelope for me? It should be easy to find as I left it on top of some papers in the middle of my desk. I need to pay Virginia for her services."

"Sure, I'll get it for you." She flashed him a phony smile.

"Sara, just a moment, I do apologize if I upset you earlier with the photos and all."

"I wish you would've asked me first before you took them. I feel like my privacy has been violated."

"Please, understand I meant no harm. Do you accept my apology?" Smiling, he placed a hand on her shoulder. She had to fight the urge to shrug it off.

"Okay, apology accepted," she said, "I'll bring you the envelope." She casually took a step backward, releasing his hand, and hurried to the study.

Sara went over to Jack's desk and found the envelope sitting on top of a stack of papers. As she picked it up, she heard a pinging sound behind her. Turning her head, she walked over to her desk.

A calendar alert had popped up on her computer. As she leaned in to read the screen, her mouth fell open. She stood frozen…petrified…she couldn't believe her eyes.

'Get out while you still can.'

Her heart pounded loudly in her ears. She couldn't

breathe. It felt as if someone were choking her. Gripping the envelope, her hands trembled as she turned from the screen.

She felt lightheaded...woozy...nauseous. The room started spinning.

All of a sudden, Jack appeared in the doorway of the study. He stood there staring at her as she stumbled toward him.

Black dots shrouded her vision, and everything grew hazy.

"Why you look as if you have seen a ghost," he said, his voice sounding far away.

In an instant, everything around her went silent.

24

"What was all the commotion?"

"She fainted."

"What happened?"

"Not sure, I sent her to the study to retrieve an envelope. She was taking too long, so I went to see what the holdup was. She was standing there, white as a sheet and then stumbled toward me and fell to the floor."

"Is she okay?"

"She is resting now."

"Should I go check on her?"

"No, you should not."

"Please don't yell, I was only asking."

"Stay out of her room, she needs her sleep. I will check on her later."

"Something happened earlier."

"What?"

"She was in here."

"Yes, I know."

"How did you know?"

"I saw her in the window."

"I was hoping she wouldn't see me."

"How the hell did she gain access?"

"You forgot to lock the door."

"I thought I could trust her."

"She took something."

"From where?"

"The box."

"What box?"

"The one in the corner…the one you forgot to seal."

"Oh dear."

"You're becoming quite forgetful these days, first the door, then the box."

"What did she take?"

"Why are those boxes still here?"

"That is irrelevant."

"You should have disposed of them."

"I need to know this very minute what she took, or you will never, ever see her again."

"No, please don't say that. You promised you wouldn't, remember?"

"For the last time, what did she take?"

"A purse."

"What purse?"

"The white purse."

25

Someone is here, standing over me.

I can't see the face. I can't open my eyes. But I can sense someone. I can feel a presence.

I can't move. My legs, my arms...I can't move them. I can't get up.

There's something heavy. It's pressing on my chest... holding me down.

It's becoming more difficult to breathe.

Help! Get off me! Help!

Sara struggled, gasping for air.

Somewhere between sleep and wakefulness, her body twitched. She took a quick breath, and her eyes blinked open. It was pitch black. She could see nothing.

Slowly lifting her hand, something soft and cottony brushed up against her fingers. She moved her legs, pulling her knees toward her chest and rolled on her side. Bracing herself with both hands, the metal coil springs in the mattress squeaked beneath her as she pushed herself upright.

As she reached out her arm, fumbling for the light switch, she knocked over the vase that stood on the nightstand. It crashed to the floor as the lights came on and shattered into pieces. She gazed down at the floor through half-slit eyes. The wilted flowers floated in a small pool of water.

Sara looked around, scanning the room. No one was there. *I could have sworn someone was here...standing over me, watching me. Was I dreaming? Was it Jack?*

She had no recollection of going to bed. She had no idea of the time of day.

Taking a deep breath, she pushed back the covers, letting out a sigh of relief when she saw herself still dressed in her sweater and jeans. Placing her feet on the wooden floor, she walked into the bathroom to grab the wastebasket and a towel. She picked up the shards of glass and flowers and tossed them in the trash.

She walked back over to the nightstand and reached for her cell phone. The time read 12:23 a.m. and the battery icon read twenty-five percent. Searching through her duffle bag for her charger, she hooked it to her phone and plugged it into the outlet.

By now Sara was fully awake, beyond exhausted, and a nervous wreck. She had thought about going back to bed, but at that point, she only wanted one thing, and it was more important than sleep. It was even more important than a chance at winning twenty-one thousand dollars. It was home. She wanted to go home. But there was just one small problem. She had no idea of the way she would get there.

Jack had reminded her of their agreement to help each other. 'A deal is a deal,' he'd said. Then he mentioned the impending snowstorm…said the roads might be closed. So surely he wouldn't be offering to drive her home anytime soon.

She thought about calling a taxi. She could tell Jack she changed her mind about the tournament, but had a strong inkling he would make it difficult for her to leave.

She also thought again about calling the police. She could tell them about her suspicions regarding Sheila's disappearance. *How does someone just vanish? Surely someone has to be missing her. Her family? Her friends? What could have happened to her? Did she really disappear?*

After being at Jack's house for a week, and becoming acquainted with him, she was aware of his temper. It upset her to see his mean-spiritedness, the way he'd treated the ducks. Sara knew if someone was cruel to an animal, that person could also be violent toward a human being. She didn't want to wait around to see if he would turn on her; she felt it was merely a matter of time.

Walking over to the window, she picked up the small wooden chair and carried it across the room, placing it in front of the door and wedging it under the doorknob. She'd had enough of Jack walking in uninvited or 'checking in on her' as he called it.

She had to figure out a way to leave without upsetting him. She needed to work on an escape plan because, in five or six hours, Jack would be up and roaming around. And the thought of being trapped in his house for one more day terrified her.

————

At 7:00 a.m. Jack was whistling as he made his way downstairs, heading toward the kitchen. He was surprised to see Sara up so early. Her back was turned to him as she stood at the sink with the water running.

"Well, there she is," he exclaimed. "Miss Sleeping Beauty."

She finished rinsing her cup and turned around. "That's funny since I haven't been sleeping much these days." She picked up the dish towel to dry her hands. "What happened last night? Did you put me to bed?"

"Of course I did. How in the world do you think you got there?" He smirked.

"Did you carry me up the stairs?"

"I did, but I was not alone." Walking over to the pot of coffee he picked up his mug. "Do you remember Virginia?"

"How could I forget? Who wouldn't remember her? She was an odd-looking lady and dressed a bit strange. She played creepy music. I swear she was trying to frighten me."

"Now, that is an unkind remark to make. Virginia was concerned about you. When you did not become conscious, she insisted on helping me put you to bed."

"When I did not regain consciousness? What do you mean?"

"You fainted last night. I do not suppose you would remember." Opening the fridge, he took out the hazelnut creamer and poured some into his cup.

"The last thing I remember was being in the study. I think I was holding something…but everything's fuzzy after that."

"Perhaps you should eat more often, to keep your strength up. I do not want you dwindling away in front of me." Raising the cup to his mouth, he caught sight of a small wastebasket by the pantry door and pointed to it. "What is that doing down here? It belongs in your bathroom."

"I brought it down. I need to empty it." She looked over at the basket and then at Jack, waiting until he took a few sips of his coffee. "I need to apologize."

"About what?" he asked, raising his eyebrows.

"The vase…the one I took upstairs…for the flowers. I knocked it over last night and it shattered."

"The cut-glass vase?" he glared at her.

"Yes, I hope it wasn't expensive."

"It was. It was a gift for my wife. But worry not. It had a large crack in it just as our marriage did."

Turning from her, he walked over to the sink and stared out the window.

"I'm sorry. It was an accident," she said, her voice quavering.

"And so it was. An accident," he mumbled under his breath.

"I'm sorry, what was that? I didn't hear you."

He spun around to face her.

"Speaking of gifts, do you not like the silver bracelet I bought for you? I noticed last night it was still in the box on top of your nightstand."

"It's lovely, thank you."

"It is lovely? Thank you? Is that all you have to say?"

"You know how I feel about gifts. I've already told you."

"Well, I bought it especially for you. It has your initial on it." He looked her straight in the eye.

"Yeah, I saw the 'S.'"

The doorbell chimed.

Jack swallowed the last of his coffee, setting the cup on the counter. He marched out of the kitchen to the foyer and opened the front door.

A sandy-haired man holding a briefcase stood before him, staring at the ground. The pumpkin had been smashed into bits and pieces, and the man didn't know where to step.

"Mr. Halvrek? Good morning, I'm Frank. I'm here to take a look at your—"

"Yes, sir, please come in."

Lifting his foot, Frank skirted around the mushy mess and crossed the threshold.

"Looks like some kids may have targeted your house. Although I wouldn't think you'd get many trick or treaters out this way," Frank said, glancing back over his shoulder.

"We seldom do. Only a few venture out this far," Jack replied. "However, someone will be quite disappointed to see her prized pumpkin in smithereens." He turned and saw Sara in the foyer glaring at him.

"What about the pumpkin? What happened?" she asked.

"I am sorry to report, but your pumpkin is no longer in one piece," he sneered.

Sara poked her head out the door and gazed at the ground.

"Who would do that?" She looked over at Frank and back at Jack. "Why would someone do that?"

"Did you forget today is Halloween?" Jack shook his head and closed the door, and then walked toward the study. Frank followed him. Sara folded her arms across her chest and trailed behind them.

"What seems to be the problem with your computer?" Frank asked, opening his briefcase on top of the table.

"It will not turn on. It is an older model, but I have not had much trouble with it…until now," Jack said, standing by his desk.

Sara went over to Frank and stuck out her hand in front of him.

"Hi, I'm Sara. We weren't properly introduced," she said,

focusing on the logo on his bright blue windbreaker. It read PC Troubleshooters.

"Hello, you must be Jack's daughter." Frank smiled as he shook her hand.

"No, I'm not," she answered curtly. "I'm here for a poker tournament, and to help him with...well, all the different things he needs help with," she added, waving her hand through the air.

"Alrighty then, I should get busy now." Frank went over to Jack's desk and tapped on the keyboard.

"You didn't tell me you were having computer issues," Sara said, gazing over at Jack.

Jack moved toward her, staring at her with deadpan eyes. "I did not tell you because I did not have the chance. Last night, after you were in here, I noticed that it would not turn on."

Frank was behind the desk and down on one knee when he looked up and over at Jack. "Excuse me, Mr. Halvrek, I found the problem with your computer."

Jack turned to him, "Yes, what is it?"

"The power cord has been cut," he said, as he stood up holding the severed cord.

"Cut?" Jack leered at Sara. "Now I wonder how that could have happened."

"Are you insinuating that I had something to do with it?" she snapped.

"Are you incriminating yourself?"

"No, I didn't touch your computer," she shot back with conviction.

"Calm down, my dear, it was just a simple question."

Frank hurried over to the table and searched through his briefcase. "Hold on, folks. Today might be your lucky day. I think I have a universal power cord somewhere in my case."

Sara couldn't help feeling as though she'd been set up. She watched as Frank tore through a tangle of cables, cords, and adapters.

Who was this Frank, the computer-fix-it man? Was this another game Jack was playing? Maybe it was a game, and Frank was in on it. Like the piano lady last night who was trying to scare her.

Virginia, the piano lady, she was in here last night. Maybe she was the one who cut the computer cord. But, no, wait, that doesn't make sense. Why would she do that? What would have been her motive? It had to have been Jack.

On one hand, Sara wasn't sure if Frank could be trusted. On the other, he could be her ticket home. She was hoping it would be *her* lucky day…hers and hers alone.

"On the way over, on the radio I heard about the snow heading our way." Frank looked up at Jack, "They were saying we could get up to three feet."

"We may be in for a doozy of a storm," Jack gazed over at Sara.

"Yeah, as soon as I'm finished here, I'll be heading back

to Englewood. Gonna try to get home before it hits," Frank said.

"Oh, is that where you live?" Sara asked. She felt a flutter of hope inside her belly.

"Yeah, I was only up here for a week helping the company with their new location," he said, pulling a long black cord from his briefcase. "This one should do the trick."

"I live in Lakewood." Sara couldn't speak the words fast enough.

"Oh, you don't say," Frank said, as he switched out the cables.

Biting her bottom lip, in an effort to contain the question simmering inside her, she couldn't resist and blurted it out. "Do you think I could hitch a ride with you?"

Frank glanced up at her but didn't say a word.

"I need to go home this weekend to pick up my car if it's not too far out of the way for you." She slowly gazed over at Jack who was eyeballing her.

"Sara, we discussed this matter the other day. Did we not? About leaving while we still have work to do."

"But my car, I can't just leave it at the dealer. They might charge me extra fees for storage and—."

"You will have all the money you need for your car repair, I promise. I will take care of it." Jack gave her a quick nod and then walked over to Frank. "How much do I owe you, my friend?"

"For the cable cord and home visit, that'll be thirty-five dollars," Frank said, closing his briefcase.

Jack pulled a hundred dollar bill from his pocket and handed it to him. "Fill up your gas tank for the ride home," he winked at him.

"Thank you, sir, I appreciate the generosity." Frank smiled and tucked the money into his jacket.

"Well, you better get moving; you have a long ride ahead of you." Jack gave Frank a quick pat on the shoulder, and they walked out of the study.

Sara stood immobile as she watched Frank leave, her chance of escape disappearing in front of her eyes. A few seconds later, she heard the front door close. Jack waltzed into the study, walking right up to her and standing inches from her face.

"You cannot leave me. You must never leave me," he said.

Backing away, she felt his stare boring into her. A grim silence fell over the room as the walls seemed to close in all around her. She felt a rising sense of panic.

Breathe, just breathe.

26

"I think she is unhappy here."

"Why?"

"She has been complaining all week how tired she is, says she is not sleeping well."

"Do you blame her? I mean, could you sleep if someone like you was around twenty-four seven?"

"What the hell is that supposed to mean?"

"You torment her."

"I do not."

"Sometimes you do."

"I do? Well, if I do, I do not mean to."

"You should be nicer to her. After all, she's only trying to help you."

"Yes, I know. However, today she ticked me off."

"What did she do?"

"Well, first, she talked badly about Virginia. You know that poor woman would not hurt a fly."

"What did she say?"

"She thought Virginia was trying to scare her with the piano music. She called it creepy."

"I'd have to agree with her on that one."

"Then she talked back to me, becoming snippy with me in front of Frank."

"Frank?"

"The computer repairman. I called him to come to the house this morning."

"I sure hope he fixed whatever was wrong with the computer. You tend to become edgy when you can't play your games."

"Yes, of course he did. I knew he would able to, it was a simple fix."

"That's a relief."

"Then she tried to finagle a ride home with Frank, right in front of me. I was standing right there watching her. She was practically begging him."

"Well, you can't keep her here forever, you know."

"I thought perhaps she would have liked it here, and would have wanted to stay."

"Maybe she's reached her breaking point. You do have a certain effect on people."

"Perhaps she has. Speaking of breaking, she broke something quite precious to me."

"What?"

"The cut-glass vase."

"Not the crystal vase, not the one you bought for…"

"Yes, that is the one. It was the last gift I gave to her the week before she—"

"Don't say it. We've been through this a million times. Remember what Dr. Moss told you…"

27

At the bottom of the stairway, Sara heard the distant sound of her cell phone ringing.

Taking the stairs, two at a time, she ran down the hallway toward her room. She rushed over to the phone still on the charger and tugged it from the wall but she missed the call.

Staring at the screen, she didn't recognize the number. Moments later, a voicemail notification popped up, and she hit the button to listen to the message.

'Hey, Sara, this is Kenny at Foxdale Audi. Your car is all fixed and ready to go. Let me know when you'll come by to pick it up. Thanks.'

Sitting on the edge of the bed, she pressed the number, holding the phone to her ear.

"Foxdale Audi, how may I direct your call?" a woman's cheery voice asked.

"Hi, service please."

"Transferring you now."

The line rang ten times before someone picked up.

"Service, this is Nate."

"Hi, is Kenny there?"

"Just a second, let me find him."

As the hold music played in her ear, she began tapping her foot along to "Take Me Home, Country Roads."

Nate's voice boomed onto the line, interrupting the song.

"Sorry, ma'am, I can't find him. He might be out on break. Would you like to leave a message?"

"I was returning his call about picking up my car. Can you let him know Sara called?"

"What's the last name?"

"Tyler. Sara Tyler."

"Will do."

"Thank you."

The line disconnected.

With the song still buzzing in her head, she had a sudden thought. *That's it! Kenny. I'll ask him to come get me. Maybe he can drive my car to me.*

A ray of hope fell upon Sara as her departure plan began to form.

Bounding down the stairs, Sara headed to the kitchen. Jack was standing at the stove.

"Just in time, lunch is ready," he said, turning to her, holding a saucepan in one hand and a ladle in the other.

Sara walked over to the table and pulled out a chair. Jack set a dish of crackers and a bowl of something orange and thick in front of her.

"What is this," she asked, scrunching up her nose, "butternut squash?"

"Of all people, I was sure you would know." He grinned. "It is pumpkin soup."

"Pumpkin? My pumpkin?" her eyes grew wide. "What did you do, scrape it off the ground, throw it in a pan, and heat it up?"

Glaring at her, he shook his head. "No, it is not your pumpkin, the one you painted the silly face on, and talked to, and mourned over. You treated that darn thing as if it had a pulse."

Sara's mouth hung open.

"You, young lady, are fruitier than that recently departed piece of fruit."

"Yeah, well, at least I have a heart and care about things… all things, living and dead."

Pushing back from the table, she sprang from the chair, squaring her shoulders. "I'd rather be fruity than an old meany like you. I saw you throwing rocks at those little ducks," she cried out, pointing to the backyard.

"Those damn ducks crap all over the yard. I did not hurt them. I was simply guiding them back to the place where they belong, in the lake." He took a step toward her. "Besides, when did you see me throwing rocks?"

She flinched, taking a step back, her back pressing up against the wall. "When did you see me talking to my pumpkin?"

Jack stood there for a moment, glowering at her and then retreated.

"Never mind," he said. "Come and sit down."

Sara stood stiff as a board, watching him. He sat down and scooped the thick soup with his spoon.

"The least you can do is taste it." Raising the spoon, he took a mouthful and swallowed. "Do not fret; it came from the store, from a can." Looking up at her, he winked and continued to eat.

"For your information, I don't like pumpkin soup," she said, sitting back down at the table. She snapped up a cracker and crunched it between her teeth.

"Sara, can I ask you something?" Placing his elbows on the table, he clasped his hands together. "Are you unhappy here?"

"What makes you ask?" Leaning over, she picked up another cracker.

"Why do you always answer my question with a question?"

"Funny, you do the same thing," she rolled her eyes. "You're always answering my questions with questions."

"Let us try this again, shall we?" Unclasping his hands, he straightened his posture. "Why were you so insistent about, how did you say it, 'hitching a ride home' with Frank?"

Sara looked down at her lap. Beneath the table, she fiddled with her paper napkin.

"Once again, are you not happy here? Do you wish to leave?" He paused. "Would you prefer to go back home and look for a job instead? Most likely it will be a dead-end job. Perhaps you would rather sit in traffic for hours and be confined to a desk all day."

Sounds better than being confined in this house.

She glanced up at him. "I just want to go home and get my car, that's all." Tiny strips of napkin rested in her lap.

"Ah yes, this matter is about your car," he said, cocking his head to the side. "I offer you an opportunity to win some money so that you can pay for your car repair, yet, as each day passes, I sense you are unhappy here and want to leave."

Picking up the napkin pieces, she held them tight in her hand. "Do you think money buys happiness?" she looked him straight in the eye.

Wetting his lips, he gave a nod of assent. "You know, there was a time when I made more money in a month than you made in a year at that former job of yours."

"Let me guess," she said. "Gambling."

His eyes flickered with amusement. "Everyone loved me

back then. They always stayed around. Never a quiet or dull moment to be had."

"So were you happy then?"

"I was lucky."

"I could use some luck right about now."

"You know what I think?" He leaped to his feet.

She gazed up at him, unsure of his next move.

"We need to turn that frown upside down. We need to lighten the mood around here and have some fun," his eyebrows danced. "We will have a little party tonight…a Halloween party. We will dress up, make some yummy snacks, and watch scary movies…just the two of us."

Sara stared at him blankly as he shimmied around the table.

"What do you say?" Looking at her, a mischievous smile was plastered on his face.

Leaning over her suitcase, Sara riffled through her clothes looking for something to wear to Jack's impromptu Halloween party.

I can't believe this nonsense…dressing up for Halloween. How old are we again?

Then she saw it. At the bottom of her suitcase, under her clothes—the white handbag. Between fainting and all the hectic activity in the house, she'd forgotten she had stashed it there.

What's with this bag anyway?

She unfastened the flap and peeked inside. She saw a hairbrush, a pack of chewing gum and something silver lying at the bottom. *Is that a piece of jewelry?* Pulling out the thin chain, she held it up and draped it over her hand.

It looked exactly like the bracelet Jack had given her, with the shiny silver charm dangling from it—the letter *'S.'*

Sheila.

The bracelet dropped to the floor as Sara covered her mouth to hold back a scream. *No! No! No!* She reached down, trembling, and picked it up. She stared at it again.

'S' for Sheila—the girl who disappeared. This bag must be hers. Her hands shook as she squeezed her eyes closed. Her mind raced to the absolute worst thought.

Unsure of her next move, she didn't know what to do. *I have to get out of here, but I can't let him know I'm leaving. I need to stay calm to get out of here alive.*

She went to the nightstand and picked up her cell phone. *No missed calls, no messages.* No one was looking for her, or missing her...yet.

Taking a deep breath, she exhaled slowly. It was getting late, and Kenny still hadn't called back. Tapping the screen, she hit the number.

"Foxdale Audi, how may I direct your call?"

"Service, please."

"Hold a moment."

"Service, this is Nate."

"Is Kenny there?"

"Can I tell him who is calling?"

"This is Sara, I called earlier. I've been waiting for him to call me back about my car."

"Hold on."

She bit her fingernails as she waited on the line.

"I can't find him. He must have left early for the weekend."

She felt a knot tighten in her stomach.

"Try back on Monday." Nate hung up before she could say anything else.

Breathe, just breathe.

Feeling light-headed, she sat down on the bed. She thought back to the day she took her car in for service.

Kenny was friendly and helpful. He seemed to understand my situation and even had the courtesy van drive me home. I remember the way he winked at me when he handed me his business card. His business card. Where did I put it?

Sara rushed over to her tote bag and unzipped the inside pocket. She found the business card tucked inside. Grasping the card, she eyed the small printed text on the front of it. Only the dealer's sales and service phone numbers and web address were listed.

Sighing, she flipped the card over and on the back was a number penned in black ink. *Oh, thank goodness.* She quickly entered the number on her phone.

"Hal-low," a husky voice answered. Sara could hear loud chattering in the background.

"Kenny?"

"You got him."

"This is Sara. Not sure if you remember me, but I dropped my car off last Friday for service."

"How could I forget the smoking hot chick with the blue A four," he said, his speech slightly slurred.

Somewhat flattered, she wasn't sure of a way to respond.

"Yes, my car is blue."

"Ohh-shun blew purrl." His words were unclear.

"Yeah, ocean blue pearl is the color." She paused. "Are you okay? Did I call at a bad time?"

"Nah, I'm just hanging with the boys, having a few brewskis. We're over here celebrating my bro's birthday."

Oh boy, he sounds drunk.

"Hey, by the way, your car is fixed and ready to go."

"Yes, that's the reason I'm calling you. Look, Kenny, I know we don't really know each other, and I'm sorry to bother you, but I could really use some help."

"Whatcha need?"

"I was wondering…well, more like hoping you could drive my car to me. I'm kind of in a tricky situation."

"Tricky huh?" he snorted.

"Not really tricky, actually, it's more of a dangerous situation."

"Dangerous? For real? You're in danger?" his voice instantly sharpened. "Hang on, let me, uh, go somewhere so I can talk."

She heard heavy footsteps clomping along and then the sound of a door shutting.

"You still there?" his voice echoed, bouncing off the walls. "I'm in the bathroom."

"Yes, as I was saying, I'm in trouble and was hoping you could either drive my car to me or pick me up and give me a ride home."

"What kinda trouble? You okay? Want me to call the police?"

"No, no, I don't want you to call the police. It's complicated. I made a bad decision. I'm at someone's house for a poker tournament, but things aren't going so well. I just need to get out of here, that's all."

"You sure you're safe? Where you at?"

"Shady Bend Lake over by Grand Lake."

"Oh yeah, I know where that is. Was there camping one time. How'd you get all the way up there?"

"It's a long story."

"Okay, want me to leave now? It might take me a few hours."

"Now? Tonight? Oh, no, you're drinking, and that wouldn't be safe, drinking and driving. Could you pick me up tomorrow?"

"Yeah, what's the address?"

"Twenty-one Shady Bend Road, but I don't think it's a good idea for you to come to the house. If you can call when you're on your way, I'll try to meet you outside nearby."

"No problem, I'd be happy to save a damsel in distress."

"I really appreciate it. I had no one else to call for help."

"Okay, hang in there."

"Thanks, Kenny, see you soon."

When he didn't reply, she realized he'd ended the call.

As she placed her phone back on the nightstand, she could hear Jack whistling as he marched down the hallway toward her room. She quickly went over to her suitcase and crouched down, stuffing the white handbag back under her clothes. Jack appeared outside her room.

"Sara, why are you not dressed for our party?" he asked, leaning against the doorway.

"Umm, I've been going through my things, but can't seem to find anything interesting to wear." Keeping her back to him, she pretended to search through her clothes.

"Well, perhaps something special is hanging in the wardrobe. I assume you have not seen it yet."

Turning toward him, she swallowed in discomfort. "No, I haven't."

"I suggest that you have a look." There was a glimmer in his eye.

She slowly stood up and ambled over to the closet.

"I do hope you like it. I will leave you to get ready, and will see you downstairs." Taking a step back, he paused, turning to her. "Oh, Sara, I almost forgot. Were you talking to someone, or am I hearing things?"

"Yeah, I was talking with my mom…checking in on her. I hadn't spoken to her in a few days."

"Very well, next time you chat with her, be sure to give her my regards," he winked and walked away.

While Sara felt bad about lying to Jack, she felt awful

when she realized it'd been a few days since she had spoken
to her mother. The days seemed to have melded into one
another, and she'd lost track of time. Soon enough she'd be
home and able to visit with her mom. She could then tell her
all about her crazy ordeal, once she escaped Jack's house.

But for now, she had to keep her escape plan secret and
had to act as if nothing had changed. Most important, she had
to work on her poker face. If she wasn't able to hide her
emotions, her chance of escaping was slim to nonexistent. So
she was going to have to fake it.

Fake it 'til you make it, as they say.

Tonight's party not only gave her the chance to fake it but
also provided a chance to be someone else, a new persona. It
would give her an opportunity to dress up in a costume, put on
a façade, and play a part.

Who will I be tonight?

She opened the closet door and gazed at a brown, faux
suede, fringed dress hanging from the rod. Reaching for the
hanger, she took out the dress and held it up in front of her.
Hooked around the top of the hanger was a multi-colored
beaded headband with a single red feather and a small, plastic
axe. Glancing at the bottom of the wardrobe, she saw a pair of
faux suede moccasins, trimmed with fringe and beads that
matched the dress.

*An Indian? I'm supposed to dress up as an Indian. Why
doesn't this surprise me?*

29

"And what are you so excited about?"

"Today is the day."

"What day?"

"I can't believe it."

"Believe what?"

"I will finally meet her."

"Calm down. I am still not a hundred percent sure I am comfortable with all this."

"What do you mean? It's been a week since she arrived."

"So."

"She is bound to find out about me sooner or later."

"I was hoping for later rather than sooner."

"But you can't keep doing this. You can't keep me hiding in here."

"She is hiding the purse in there."

"In where?"

"Her room."

"You didn't ask her about it yet?"

"When I went to put the costume in her closet, I looked all around, but did not find it."

"What costume?"

"The one for our little party tonight."

"You're having a party? Who else did you invite?"

"No one else, it will be just the two of us."

"Then I certainly have to meet her tonight."

"And why is that?"

"I have the perfect costume."

"I am sure you have quite the collection; however, I almost forgot to mention…"

"What?"

"I heard her talking to someone on the phone."

"What was she saying?"

"I heard her say, 'see you soon.' When I asked who she was talking to, she said it was her mother."

"Then maybe it was her mother."

"I do not believe her. I have a sneaking suspicion she is making plans to leave."

"No, she can't leave. I haven't met her yet."

"Oh quit your damn whining."

"Let me come to the party tonight, please? I'm dying to meet her."

"The more I think about it, you should stay here. It is much safer here."

"No, I want to come to the party."

"No, I have decided that you will stay here. This party will only be for the two of us."

"Oh no, it won't. Your little party will be a party for three. You just wait and see."

30

Standing in front of the bathroom mirror, Sara adjusted the headband on her forehead. It wouldn't stay put and kept riding up on the back of her head. Stray pieces of hair were catching on the beads as she repositioned the feather.

This hairdo does not go with this headpiece. She tore off the headband and threw it on the counter.

Rummaging through her cosmetic travel case, she pulled out two elastic hair ties. She wet her brush and brushed her hair until it was smooth. She parted her hair down the middle and styled it into two long braids.

After placing the headband back on her head, it no longer tugged on her hair. As she leaned in closer to the mirror, she ran her fingers under her bloodshot eyes. *Ugh, I look terrible.*

A week of sleepless nights had taken its toll.

She walked over to the wardrobe and slipped her feet into

the moccasins. They fit a little snug, but she would have to deal with them pinching her toes for a few hours to appease Jack. Eyeing the plastic axe on the bed, she picked it up, raised her hand, and sliced it through the air.

If he comes near me, I'll fend him off with my mini-hatchet. A wicked laugh escaped from her throat.

Descending the stairs, Sara padded along toward the kitchen, sniffing the air. Something was burning.

Tossing the axe on the counter, she rushed to the oven and opened the door. Smoke billowed out as she reached for the dish towel. Quickly wrapping the towel around her hand, she grabbed at the metal tray and pulled it out from the oven.

"Ouch," she yelped, dropping the tray on top of the stove. The cheese was still bubbling on the charred-edged pizza in front of her.

Pepperoni... how gross. And it looks like it's breathing.

"Are you in there?" Jack called out. He came striding toward the kitchen, his boots jangling. "Are you okay? What is going on?"

Walking over to the stove, he inspected the tray.

"Hope you like it extra crispy. The pizza got burned, and so did I," she said, holding up her index finger.

Jack opened the freezer and plopped two ice cubes in a cup. "Here, this will help with the swelling."

Taking the cup from him, Sara stuck her finger inside and leaned back against the counter.

"I must say, injured finger and all, you are as pretty as a picture."

Oh no, no more pictures, please. Not in this costume.

"You look like a beautiful tribal princess." Jack cast a wandering eye, grinning from ear to ear. The way he was staring made her cringe.

Poker face, remember the poker face. Time to play the game and act the part. You need to be cool, calm, collected. Fake it 'til you make it. Fake it 'til you make it out of here.

"Thank you." She flashed him a feigned smile. "Now let me guess, you're a cowboy."

"How did you ever figure it out? Did the spurs on my boots give it away?"

"Actually, it was the hat."

Jack tipped his black Stetson to her and then loosened the red bandana around his neck. A black leather eye patch covered his right eye. He was wearing his signature western shirt with a black suede vest and black jeans. On his hip, strapped to his belt, was a tooled leather holster. Tucked inside it was his handgun.

Sara couldn't help staring at his gun. It was the closest she had ever been to a weapon.

"That's a pretty fancy holster you have," she remarked.

"Oh, this old thing," he patted it twice. "I have had it forever. It was custom-made to fit my six-shooter."

"Six-shooter? Is that what it's called?"

"Yes, ma'am. A Colt Single Action," he said, as he drew it from his holster.

"Single action?" Her heart rate sped up as she took a step back, keeping her gaze glued to him.

"Yes, it is an 1873 Single Action Army."

"It looks like one of those guns you'd see in an old Western."

"Yes, it does, would you like to hold it?"

"N-no, no thanks," she took another step back, raising her hands in front of her.

"Relax," he said, sliding it back into his holster. "It is also known as the Peacemaker," he winked.

Taking a deep breath, she exhaled and then swallowed.

"Wait until you see the way I decorated for our party." Smiling at her, he turned away and headed for the living room.

Setting the cup of ice on the counter, Sara picked up the plastic axe and followed him.

The first thing she noticed upon entering the room was the fireplace. Draped with a black, netted gauze, hairy black spiders clung to the fabric and appeared to be climbing the wall. On top of the mantel was an assortment of foam figurines: witches, skeletons, and vampires.

Inside the fireplace, ten white pillar candles, all glowing, were set in a row. Jack had placed two chairs in front of the fireplace with the side table positioned between them. A large plastic crow sat perched on the table, guarding a bowl filled with candy corn.

"Wow, I would never have thought you'd have all these decorations," she said.

"Yes, well, I found them stashed away in a box in the garage. I had forgotten all about them. It has been years since they have been displayed. My wife used to decorate for every holiday." Plucking two pieces of candy corn from the bowl, he chewed them.

"Shall we enjoy some cocktails?" he asked.

Lifting the stopper from the glass decanter, he poured some of its contents into a martini glass. He then reached for a tiny plastic bottle on the table and flipped open the lid, shaking a few drops of the dark liquid into the drink. Handing her the glass, she saw swirls of black floating among the clear liquid. It looked as if a black ink pen had exploded inside the drink.

"This looks interesting," she narrowed her eyes. "What is it?"

"That would be a black widow. My wife collected recipes for various occasions. It called for dark rum, but I did not have any, so I added a little food coloring to make it festive."

"Where the heck did you find black food coloring? I've never seen it before." Inspecting the glass, she placed it on the table.

"Oh, I found it in the box with the other holiday ornaments."

After watching the drops of food coloring twirl and sink to the bottom of her glass, Sara glanced over at Jack as he stirred his drink, turning it black.

"Did you make this with real rum?"

"Yes."

"Really? I thought you didn't drink alcohol."

"Normally I do not. But I thought, what the hell, one little cocktail for our party will not hurt us, will it?" Walking over to her, he held up his glass.

"Let us toast, to a sweet girl named Sara."

Setting the plastic axe on the table, she lifted her glass to him and smiled her best fake smile.

"Never bring a knife to a gunfight," he clinked her glass.

"Knife?" She giggled. "It's not a knife. It's an axe."

"Actually, it is a tomahawk."

"Axe, tomahawk. Tomato, tomahto."

"Speaking of tomatoes, I will serve the pizza." He set his glass on the table and strode away.

Sara walked to the fireplace to check out the decorations on the mantel. Tucked in the corner, hidden behind a vampire figure, were the photos Jack had taken of her. The frames were stacked on top of each other, face down.

Not wanting to think about them and upset herself again, she focused on the candles below, their flames flickering and dancing inside the fireplace. She took a deep breath and then sipped her drink.

Jack returned with the pizza and two plates on the tarnished tray and set it on the table. He took his seat and grabbed a slice. Taking another sip of her drink, Sara sat down to join him.

"Are you hungry yet?" he asked. Sinking his teeth into his slice of pizza he chewed it loudly.

"It has pepperoni on it." Her lips curled in disgust.

"And?"

"And I don't eat meat."

"Well, just remove it and give it to me." Lifting his plate, he waved it in front of her.

"An animal is not an it. An animal is a she, a he, or a who."

"Oh, quit your darn fussing and drop that she or he or whoever it was onto my plate."

Pulling a slice off the tray, one by one she picked off the pieces of pepperoni and planted them on his dish.

"They have souls, you know," she said, her tone sharp, warning him. Staring down at her slice full of cheese-less holes, she grimaced.

"Happy now?" He popped a piece of pepperoni in his mouth.

"No. It makes me sad that a poor little pig had to be slaughtered."

"Well, if you are going to be sad, do not forget to mourn the poor cow, too. In case you are unaware, this tasty meat is made from both animals."

After popping another piece of pepperoni in his mouth, he

polished off the last bite of his pizza, washing it down with his cocktail.

"Can we please stop talking about dead animals?" On the verge of tears, she looked away, shaking her head.

"No wonder you were so upset about the moose head and the ducks," he said.

Sara took a tiny bite of her crust and swallowed. *No, no, not the ducks again.* She reached for her drink.

"I am terribly sorry about the ducks and the rocks. Those creatures make their nests in my backyard. The eggs, their darling babies, are so fragile." Jack cupped his hands as if he were cradling an egg. "They need to be protected."

Sara glanced at him over her martini glass as she gulped it.

"I did not hurt them. You must understand." Rising to his feet, he faced her and stared into her eyes. "I would never hurt them. I would never hurt anyone." A tear trickled down his cheek.

Sara wasn't sure what to think but had a sinking feeling in her stomach. Was he defending himself? Was he trying to convince her he had nothing to do with Sheila's disappearance?

Poker face, remember the poker face. Keep cool, take a deep breath. She mustered up all of the strength she could to remain calm and collected.

"I think we need another drink." Picking up her martini

glass, she gave it a quick shake. "What was the name of it again?"

"A black widow," he mumbled, running a finger under his nose.

"That's right. Well, I'm calling mine empty," she said. "Show me the way to make them, will you?"

Sara shot up from the chair and went into the kitchen to get more ice. She would be sure to water down her drinks. Jack's martinis, however, would soon be doubled.

Two hours and three rounds of drinks later, Sara was intrigued by Jack's childhood stories.

"So…your real name isn't Jack?"

"No, I am afraid not. It is Oliver. My birth name is Oliver," he said, removing his hat and placing it on the floor beside him.

"Why did you change it? Oliver is a nice name."

"Well, you see, back in the day, when I was a kid, we used to play a game called cowboys and Indians."

"Hmm, I never would've guessed," she said, in a sarcastic tone.

"We would split up into two groups and divide the backyard into two territories. One side would be the cowboys, and the other side the Indians. I would always be a cowboy of course."

"Of course," she nodded in agreement.

"The object of the game was to defend your territory and stay hidden from the other team until you attack."

"Attack?"

"No one ever got hurt, it was harmless. Back then it was all in good fun. The Indians use to pretend to hold bows and arrow like this, and the cowboys pointed their fingers like this…with their imaginary pistols. It was then when they decided to nickname me."

"What was your nickname?"

"Well, being a cowboy, they started calling me 'Oliver with the revolver.' I just shrugged it off, but the name followed me through school."

"So when did you change your name?"

"After I lost my eye."

"You lost an eye?" she gasped, dumbfounded.

"Yes, my right eye is made of glass. I thought you knew, or at least had figured it out by now."

"How?" A lump formed in Sara's throat. "How did it happen?"

"Bar fight, many years ago."

"Oh no."

"Oh yes, I was clocked in the head."

"Yikes," she winced.

"Bunch of us were playing cards that day in our usual spot on a Sunday afternoon. An argument broke out at the bar. We could hear the ruckus from our corner table. Some tough guy was harassing the drunk sitting next to him. They were both rowdy and swearing. So I stood up, put my cards on the table, and walked over to him. I told him to keep it down and told him it was rude to be cussing in front of a lady."

"Then what happened?"

"Then he started in on me, telling me to mind my business. I had invited the gal over to our table, to move her away from them to keep her safe. Well, then he stood up, facing me. Maybe he thought I was trying to steal his gal. The bastard was holding a damn shot glass when he punched me. It shattered in my face, puncturing my eye."

"Ouch, that must have been so painful," she said, squinting her eyes.

"That was the day I lost my eye and found my wife."

"Found your wife?" There was a momentary pause. "Wait...do you mean the girl at the bar? You married her?"

"Well, not that day of course, but yes. That is the way we met."

"So, hold on a sec, I'm a bit confused...let me get this straight. You changed your name when you met the girl at the bar who later became your wife?"

"I suppose one could look at it that way."

"Could you please explain it a bit more?"

"Well, you see, right before the guy hit me, my buddy yelled 'blackjack.' We were playing twenty-one that day. Apparently Sylvia, the gal who later became my wife, only heard part of it and she thought he was calling my name.

When I dropped to the floor, covering my eye, she leaned down over me. I remember she kept saying it, over and over, in that sweet, soft voice of hers. 'Jack, can you hear me? Jack, do you need a doctor?' She looked like an angel floating over me, so caring and concerned. At that point, I did not want to correct her, so I let her call me by that name."

"Oh, wow, what a love story."

"Yes, well, it was short lived. Soon after that, after she became acquainted with me, she called me one-eyed Jack."

"Why did she call you that?" Sara frowned. "It sounds mean, considering your injury and all."

"That, my dear, is another story for a different day. Perhaps we should change the subject now." Untying the bandana, he removed it from his neck and stuffed it into his back pocket.

"But it's interesting to hear about your life and all. Just one more story…please?" She smiled.

"Oh all right, twist my arm, young lady, one more, and that will be all."

"Okay."

"In a standard deck of playing cards, there are three face cards that only show one eye. They are the king of diamonds, the jack of hearts, and the jack of spades."

"Oh, the jack of spades, the screen name you use on the poker site."

"Yes, it is," he said. Running his fingers under the strap of his eyepatch, he massaged his temple. "Anyway, in regard to the two jack cards, hearts and spades, Sylvia, my wife, used to chide me, or rather, make snide comments."

"Chide you? Make snide comments? How do you mean?"

"Well, when we got along, she would call me her Jack of hearts. But when we quarreled, she would call me Jack of spades."

"But all couples have their ups and downs, their good and bad days."

"That is what I tried to tell her. That is what I always tried to tell her. But she would not listen." Holding her gaze, he picked up his glass, sipped the dark beverage and then placed it on the table.

"Would you mind going to the kitchen and bringing in our dessert? The cupcakes should be thawed by now. I took them out of the freezer hours ago."

"Sure, be right back." Sara rose to her feet and headed to the kitchen.

Jack pushed himself out of the chair and stood in front of the mantel. Moving the decorations aside, he picked up the picture frames with the photos of Sara, setting them upright. He smiled as he gazed longingly at each one.

"What would I do without you my dear?" he whispered under his breath.

Moments later, Sara returned. "Here we go, two instant sugar rushes coming up."

Setting the cupcakes on the table, she studied them. Each

mini-cake had white frosting smashed down on it with two chocolate chips on top.

"Are these, or should I say, were these supposed to be ghosts?" she asked.

"I suppose so." Reaching for a cupcake, he peeled away the paper liner. "They looked quite different when they were fresh."

"Do you believe in ghosts?"

"When I was a young boy, I was afraid of ghosts. But as I grew older, I realized people can be much scarier."

Licking off all the frosting, he bit into the chocolate cake, devouring it in three mouthfuls.

"It is time for our movie," he said, brushing the crumbs from his shirt. He walked over to the TV and picked up the remote. "So what shall we watch, a Western or something scary?"

"You like old Westerns, don't you? I heard you watching one earlier this week."

"Those were the good old days...the days of good movies with great stories. Not like the rubbish they show nowadays. Many of my favorites were filmed in the 1940s, and '50s. I love to watch them for the clever dialogue they had. They do not make movies like they used to, that is for sure."

Clicking through the channels, he stopped on a local news station and watched for a few minutes to catch up on the news. A weather alert flashed along the bottom of the screen. As he turned up the volume, Sara walked over next to him.

They stood, transfixed, in front of the TV as the weatherman's voice forecasted.

"A winter storm warning is in effect for Grand County and surrounding areas. The storm is expected to arrive early Saturday morning and continue into Sunday, with accumulations of twenty-four to thirty-six inches in some areas, causing potentially hazardous driving conditions. Stay tuned for more updates in your local area."

"Well, it looks like we will be canceling the tournament this weekend. We will have to reschedule it for another time. I am glad we stocked up on supplies though. We could be snowed in for a while." Gazing at Sara, he detected uncertainty in her eyes.

"Yeah, it's a good thing we did," she said, trying to hide her fear.

"Perhaps we should watch an old horror flick. It is Halloween after all." He shot her a sideways glance.

Thumbing through the buttons on the remote, Jack scrolled through the listing guide. Halfway down, he paused. "I think I have found our movie for the evening. It starts in five minutes."

"You sure you want to watch a movie," she said, stifling a yawn. "It's getting kind of late."

"Are you going to be a spoilsport?"

"I'm not trying to be, but don't you usually go to bed by now?"

"Yes, but tonight is our night...it is a special night. You

have been here almost a week, and that in itself is cause for celebration."

"I thought you said this was a Halloween party."

"Can it not be a little of both?" he winked at her.

"I guess."

"Well, if you do not want to watch a movie, what would you prefer to do?"

"I liked hearing your stories, particularly the one about the way you met your wife."

Removing his eyepatch, he massaged his brow.

"May I ask what happened to her?"

He looked down for a few seconds and then lifted his head.

"She passed away."

"Oh, I'm so sorry to hear that."

"It happened long ago."

"Was she sick?"

"No," he said, gazing down. "She was not ill."

"Do you have any children?"

"Okay, Sara, that is enough," he turned away. "I am putting an end to all this storytelling."

"I'm sorry. I meant no harm. Please know that if you ever need or want to talk about anything, you can talk to me."

"I do not need to talk to you or anyone else for that matter. This party is officially over," he snapped.

"Yeah, it's late, time to call it a night," she said, unable to disguise the troubled note in her voice.

She walked back to the table, put the dishes and martini glasses on the tray and hurried to the kitchen.

As she placed the tray on the counter, the lights flickered. She went over to the sink and peered out the window. A cluster of dark clouds hung low in the night sky. She gazed in the direction of the pitch black lake. A cold chill crept over her.

The lights flickered again, longer this time. She drew in a quick breath. Moments later, darkness fell inside the house.

The power had gone out.

"Oh, Sara, where are you?" Jack's voice called for her.

Sara remained silent as she stood by the sink, clinging to the edge of the counter, petrified.

"Come out, come out, wherever you are."

She swallowed hard, her entire body rigid with fear.

"I have a candle for you."

She turned and saw two small flames, side by side, slowly heading toward her. As the flames came closer, she saw Jack's illuminated face inches from hers.

"Why I almost walked right into you," he said, handing her a pillar candle. "Why did you not answer me?"

"Th-thanks, what happened?" her voice wavered.

"I am uncertain. I will need to check the circuit breaker. Stay put. I will return shortly."

Jack turned away, the single flame gliding through the air

until he opened the door that connected with the garage. Sara didn't move an inch. With both hands wrapped around the candle, she waited, listening to his every step as he shuffled around in the garage.

Please tell me this is another one of his games. Halloween night and the lights go out. This can't be real. He might be trying to scare me again.

The door opened and closed. A bright beam of light shone straight into the kitchen.

"I have my flashlight now, we are good."

"Is the power out here or everywhere?" she asked.

"While I am quite sure it is not out everywhere, I am sure it is out here."

"Do any of the neighbors have power?"

"Well, let me check."

With the ray of light streaming in front of him, he walked over to the back door. Unlocking and opening it, he stepped onto the deck. Sara moved toward the half-opened door and looked for herself. He quickly turned around, closed the door and locked it again.

"There is nothing but blackness all across the lake, so I will assume the entire community has no power." He reached out and took hold of her arm.

"Since there is nothing more to see here, I will guide us upstairs," he said.

"It's okay. I can find my way. I'll just take this candle with me and go slow."

"Sara, now is not the time to be difficult." She felt his nails digging into her as his grip tightened on her arm.

She cupped her hand around the flame while Jack beamed the flashlight in front of them. They slowly made their way out of the kitchen.

"We only see where we shine the light; everything else is darkness," he said, as they plodded along. "Yet so much more exists all around us, so much more we cannot see."

Jack led her up the stairs, down the hallway, and to her room.

"Well, this is my stop." On edge, she was ready to move away from him.

"I am sure the power will be restored by morning, and all will be back to normal."

"I hope so," she said, reaching for the doorknob.

"I know you have not been sleeping well, but try to get some rest. Tomorrow is Saturday, so perhaps you can sleep in a bit later."

Saturday, my escape day. I'll be able to sleep more soundly when I get home.

"Oh, and please be sure to extinguish that candle before you fall asleep. I would not want you burning the house down."

A vision of Jack's house erupting in flames entered her mind. *That would be one way to escape. If the house burns down, maybe some firemen could save me.*

"I'll be sure," she replied. "It's half melted anyhow."

Opening the door, she closed it behind her and leaned against it. She could hear the jangle of Jack's spurs fade away as he headed down the hallway.

She released a long sigh and went over to the nightstand. Setting the candle down, she reached for her phone. It was 9:35 p.m.

She tapped on the web browser icon and was about to type the name 'Oliver Halvrek' in the search bar. The screen read 'No Service.' She glanced at the battery icon.

How can there only be forty-three percent left? I just charged this thing this morning.

She couldn't risk having the battery die, Kenny would be calling her in the morning to arrange their meeting place. So she turned off her phone and placed it back on the nightstand.

She carefully walked over to the window and stared out toward the lake. *Jack was right. Nothing but complete blackness.* She shuddered as an eerie feeling coursed through her body. Tugging at the curtains, she drew them back as far as possible. She wanted to be sure they were open when morning arrived. Daylight couldn't come soon enough.

She picked up the candle to take into the bathroom. The flame swayed and almost went out. She took off her costume and reached for her pajamas hanging on the back of the door.

After slipping into them, she went through the drawers and cabinets, searching for matches. *Nothing.* Not that she had expected to find any. At that moment she wished she hadn't stopped collecting matchbooks.

Although Sara never smoked a day in her life, she used to collect matchbooks as souvenirs. When she went on vacation, she would take them from local bars and restaurants. Instead of collecting seashells from the beach, she collected matchbooks from all the places she visited. She would take them home and put them in a glass jar as mementos of her travels. Since it had been six years since her last vacation, she was certain she had no matches in her tote bag.

She went over to the door that connected to the adjacent bedroom and jiggled the handle. *It's still locked, good.* Lifting the candle from the counter, she made her way back to the bed and set it on the nightstand.

She pulled back the quilt and climbed under the covers. As she put her head on the pillow, she gazed at the candle. The flame danced alone in the darkness.

If I blow it out now, that'll be it. No more light until morning.

'Please be sure to extinguish that candle before you fall asleep. I would not want you burning the house down.' She could hear Jack's voice as if he were whispering in her ear.

How come I have the candle, and he has the flashlight? I'm sure he has more than one of them in this house. And then she remembered. *The flashlight. Where did I see it?* She scanned her tired brain. *His car, it was under his seat, I remember I found it...I was holding it.*

She threw back the covers and slowly went to her tote bag hooked on the back of the chair. Sticking her arm inside her bag, she felt around all the items. Then she touched it: cold, hard, cylindrical. *The flashlight.* Grasping it, she pulled it out from her tote and crawled back into bed, inching her way over near the nightstand.

How does this thing turn on? Holding it near the candle, she clicked the push button with her thumb. *Wow, this is extra bright.* She was elated.

Before I forget... She climbed out of bed, flashlight in hand, and walked over to the small chair. As she placed it under the doorknob, she was hoping it would be the last night she had to use a protective barrier. She was hoping to be back home, safe in her apartment by nightfall the following day.

On her way back to bed, she leaned over the candle and blew out the flame with one quick breath. Clutching the flashlight, she tucked her hand under her pillow.

I can't let him know I have this, or he might take it from me. If the power doesn't come back on, I'll need it tomorrow when I escape.

Closing her eyes, her thoughts drifted, envisioning the phone call from Kenny in the morning. Then a wave of trepidation washed over her.

Oh no. What if Kenny forgets to pick me up? He may have already forgotten our conversation. He was half drunk when we spoke on the phone. How the heck am I going to get out of here? Jack watches my every move.

Sara was so immersed in her thoughts, she had failed to make a solid game plan.

What if the power isn't restored? What if my phone battery dies? What if the snow is so deep I can't get out? I could be confined here for days, weeks...imprisoned in this house.

The sudden sound of a helicopter buzzed overhead, cutting through the silence of the night. Switching on the flashlight, she swung her legs over the side of the bed and went to the window.

Through the veil of darkness, a ray of light shone down from the sky. She stood by the window as the helicopter circled around, scanning the area with its searchlight.

I wonder what they're looking for.

Her thoughts crept back to that day by the lake, the day she saw something floating near the surface. *What if there really was a body in the lake? What if it's Sheila?* The helicopter circled one last time before disappearing into clouds.

Sara felt a sharp pang in her heart. She took a deep breath and slowly made her way back to bed. Raising her knees to her chest, she wrapped her arms around them and rocked back and forth, trying to comfort herself. *Breathe, just breathe.*

With the flashlight still clenched in her hand, she curled up onto her side and cried herself to sleep.

33

"Have you been drinking?"

"Why do you ask?"

"I can smell it on your breath."

"I had a drink or two, so what."

"You seem a bit grumpy. Did something happen at your little party?"

"It was going swimmingly until she started grilling me about Sylvia."

"How does she know about her?"

"Well, I suppose some of it is my fault. I began telling her stories about my childhood, and then one thing led to another and…"

"Did you tell her what happened?"

"No, I did not divulge that information. Now please stop interrupting."

"Go on."

"As I was saying, one thing led to another, and I told her the story about the night I met Sylvia."

"So she does know what happened."

"No, I just said she does not."

"How did you stop yourself from letting it slip out?"

"I simply told her the party was over."

"What did she say? What did she do?"

"She ran off to the kitchen. I think I may have upset her when I raised my voice."

"You need to stop raising your voice, and stop trying to scare her."

"Perhaps she was afraid because the lights went out."

"You mean because you turned them off."

"Why are you not listening? I said, The. Lights. Went. Out. There is a power outage."

"What happened?"

"Hell if I know."

"So now there's no power."

"That is correct."

"And there's a snowstorm on the way."

"Also correct. That is what I heard when listening to the news."

"What about the tournament?"

"Unfortunately, it will have to be canceled. There will be no others arriving this weekend."

"Or departing for that matter."

"What do you mean?"

"Well, if we get snowed in, Sara won't be leaving anytime soon."

34

When Sara opened her eyes, she was shivering from head to toe. An icy draft whirled around her, the room feeling like an icebox. She slowly sat up, reaching for the blanket at the end of the bed and draped it over her shoulders. As she wrapped the blanket tightly around her torso, she gazed out the window. She watched as snow sprinkled down from a gray, dismal sky.

Turning toward the nightstand, she grabbed her cell phone and powered it on. The time was 7:10 a.m., and the battery read thirty-nine percent. She zeroed in on the date for a moment.

Saturday, November first. My last day at Jack's house.

She rolled out of bed, pulled on her jeans, and layered herself with three tops: a long-sleeved cotton shirt, a lightweight sweater, and her fleece jacket. Eyeing the moccasin booties by the bed, she pulled them on. They provided a little more warmth than her thin soled ballet flats.

Picking up her phone, she made sure it was on vibrate and slipped it into her jacket pocket. She went into the bathroom and flicked the light switch. Nothing happened. The power was still out.

Through swollen eyes, she caught a glimpse of herself in the mirror. She barely recognized the face staring back at her. Despite the few hours of sleep she had gotten, she was ready to drop. She felt emotionally drained from being around Jack all week.

Dealing with him was no easy task, he had exhausted her mentally, pushing her beyond her limits. She couldn't wait to go home to her quiet little apartment and return to her normal and boring routine.

She undid her two braids and ran a brush through her hair, tying it back into a crimped, wavy ponytail. While still unsure of the manner in which she was going to escape from the house, she was eager to speak with Kenny. She figured she'd give him another hour or two, and if he didn't call her, she'd call him. Her stomach growled, momentarily interrupting her train of thought. The sugary treats she had consumed the night before had left her hungrier than usual.

She removed the chair from under the doorknob and placed it alongside the wall. Opening the door, she poked her head out and peeked down the hallway. Jack's bedroom door was closed, as expected. No music and no clanging of pans echoed through the house. All was quiet.

Trying to make as little noise as possible, she crept down the hall and the stairs. When she rounded the corner, she saw Jack sitting in the living room by the fireplace where a fire was burning at a good rate. He was still dressed in his cowboy getup from the night before, boots, spurs, gun, and all. As she walked over to him, she wondered if he'd even been to bed.

"Good morning," she said. "Looks like the power is still out."

"Care for some instant breakfast?" he asked, not looking up at her.

"Instant breakfast?" she sat down in the chair beside him.

Lifting a saucepan from the floor, he plopped a generous serving of lumpy oatmeal into a bowl and passed it to her.

"I cooked it over the fire," he said, placing the pan back on the floor. He then reached for the coffee pot and poured strong coffee into a cup. "It is not as good as the gourmet roasted beans, but it will suffice." His voice sounded gravelly. "Instant oatmeal plus instant coffee equals instant breakfast."

Leaning back into his chair, he slowly sipped from his cup. He still hadn't made eye contact with her.

Sara sensed a strange vibe emanating from Jack. He wasn't acting his usual quirky self. Something was bothering him. He looked haggard and forlorn. His sullen mood matched the dreary weather.

"Well, it looks as though winter has arrived," he said,

glancing at her. "The snow has started to fall, and I need to park the Caddy inside the garage. It is sitting outside in the driveway."

Sara took a bite of the cold, sticky oatmeal, swallowed it, and gazed at Jack. He was tapping his fingers on the side of his mug.

"Do you happen to know where my key is?" he asked. "For the life of me, I cannot seem to find it." Rising from the chair, he added another log to the fire.

"Key? No, you never gave me any keys," she replied, shaking her head.

"Hmm, is that so? Then how did you drive the Caddy to the automotive shop the other day?"

"Oh, you mean the keys to the car."

"That would be the one," he sighed.

"I thought I gave them back to you when we came home."

"Well, apparently, you thought wrong, I have looked everywhere."

"Maybe you misplaced them."

"No, I did not misplace 'them.' There is no 'them.' There is only 'one.'" Infuriated, he raised his finger in the air and yelled, "'One' key for the Caddy."

"I just told you, I don't have it." Her phone vibrated against her side.

"Well, I am telling you right now, you better find it."

"But I don't even know where to look."

Pulling her phone halfway out of her pocket, she glanced at the number. *Please let this be Kenny.*

"Do you take that damn phone with you everywhere you go?"

Her hands trembled as she quickly stuffed her phone back into her pocket and got up from the chair.

"Why I ought to take that thing away from you and throw it in the lake." Placing his hand on his holster, he glared at her.

"No, please, don't. It's my only way to stay in touch with my mom," she said, tears filling her eyes.

"Go to your room," he shouted harshly.

Her phone vibrated again. Sliding her hand into her pocket, she held it tight. She wanted to answer it and scream for help...but the look in Jack's eye told her not to chance it. He was seething with anger. With one hand hovering over his gun and the other by his side, he was ready and waiting... ready to reach out and snatch the phone from her.

"Do you not listen?" he walked toward her.

Taking a step back, she swallowed, holding his gaze.

"I said go to your room, now. Stop what you are doing and go upstairs this instant. Do not come out until you find that key."

With her heart climbing to her throat, Sara ran out of the living room, high-tailing it up the stairs. She bolted down the hallway to her room and slammed the door. Grabbing the chair, she shoved it under the doorknob.

This is insane. I have to get out of here. She whipped out her cell phone and tapped on the missed call.

"Hello."

"K-Kenny?" she stuttered.

"Yeah, who's this?"

"It's S-Sara...did you just call me?"

"Yeah, hey, are you okay? You don't sound so good."

"Please tell me you're on your way. Jack just came unglued, yelling at me."

"Did he hurt you?"

"No, not yet."

"What do mean not yet? What happened?"

"He carries a gun. I need to get away from here, and I'm afraid he won't let me leave."

"Sara, I think you should call the police."

"No, no, you don't understand. He'll just send them away, like the others...as he always does. He's an expert at charming people. He twists things around and then pretends everything's okay. I've tried to leave, but he makes it really hard. He's scaring me...he said I must never leave."

"Okay, calm down, calm down, and take a deep breath."

"When can you get here?"

"I should be there by noon. I just woke up a little while ago, didn't get much sleep, had a late night."

"Yeah, well, join the sleepless nights club. I haven't gotten a decent night's sleep in a week."

"Wow, sounds like you're having a rough time."

"That's putting it mildly…to top it off, the power went out last night, and it's still out."

"What happened?"

"I don't know, but now it's snowing, just started this morning."

"Okay, like I said, depending on the road conditions, I should be there around noon. What was the address again?"

"Twenty-one Shady Bend Road at the lake."

"Oh yeah, I remember putting it in my phone last night, so I wouldn't forget."

"What kind of car are you driving?"

"I'll be in a…so I'll…"

There was static on the line, his voice cutting in and out.

"Kenny? Kenny? Can you hear me?"

More static.

"Are you still there?"

They were cut off.

Tucking her phone into her jacket, she let out a breath and walked over to the window. The snow was coming down faster now in big heavy flakes.

Why does Jack think I have his car key? She stared out toward the lake. *I drove his car once, with that keyless push button start. Wait a minute…that key. That key fob he gave me.*

She reached for her tote bag, emptied it on the bed, and ran her hands through all her personal items. There was no key fob.

Glancing around the room, she tried to remember what she was wearing the day she drove his car. She opened the wardrobe and stuck her hand into the pocket of the powder blue coat. She felt something. *I do have it.*

Pulling it out, she held it in her hand. The key fob, a single key hanging from it. As she looked closer at the key, she saw a faded letter written on it. *Is that the letter 'G?'*

Sitting on the bed, she stuffed her items back into her tote bag. *'G?' 'G' as in garage?* Her pulse quickened. *Is this the key to the door that connects to the garage? Oh please, please, I hope so...because this is the way I'm going to escape.*

Her moment of joy was soon interrupted with a dose of reality.

How the heck am I even going to get ten feet from that door without him seeing me? Him and that hawk-eye of his... always watching me. And now he's angry, thinking I lost his key. If he finds out I have it, he'll think I've been hiding it all along.

Gritting her teeth, she wanted to scream, not at Jack and not for help. She wanted to scream at herself for letting things get this far. She should never have agreed to help him with the tournament. She should have heeded all of the warning signs from the beginning, from the very second he'd messaged her.

But Sara had a difficult time saying no to people, especially to those in need of help. She had a feeling that there was something more going on with Jack. She sensed he was hurting and hiding behind some sort of pain. He seemed troubled by something, but from what exactly, she was unsure. Loneliness? The loss of his wife?

She got up from the bed and gazed out the window. The snow was coming down hard, and there were already a few inches on the ground. If it continued falling as fast as it was, there'd be close to a foot by the time Kenny arrived.

Think Sara, think. How the hell are you going to escape from this place?

35

One thing Sara knew for certain was that she would have to leave her suitcase behind. No way would she be able to escape Jack's house with all her bags. She would have to leave most of her clothes and personal items behind.

That must be the reason he has all that luggage...from all the girls who escaped.

In her mind she could picture them all fleeing his house, racing down the road, with only the clothes on their backs. But what about the girls who weren't so lucky? The ones who didn't escape...like Sheila who supposedly vanished. It was beyond tragic. *That poor girl's body could be at the bottom of the lake.*

Sara shook the frightening thought from her mind and walked over to her suitcase. Picking out her most valuable items, she set them aside. She was already wearing her favorite jeans and three layered tops. She decided whatever she could fit into her duffle bag and her tote without being weighed down would go.

There was a knock on her door.

She went over and removed the wedged chair from under the knob. Sliding it to the side, she took a deep breath and opened the door.

"I thought by now you might be ready for lunch," Jack said, holding the tarnished silver tray. "You hardly ate any of your breakfast."

"Thank you," she replied, taking the tray from him. She set it down on the chair.

"What is that doing there?" he asked, pointing to the chair. "It belongs over by the window."

"Oh, I just put it there so I could keep my coat and handbag within reach."

"But neither your coat nor handbag is setting on it," he said, narrowing his eyes.

"Yeah, well, when we were going in and out, running errands and all, I kept my belongings in one place for easy access."

"Funny, it is the first time I noticed it there."

Sara watched as he slowly gazed around the room. She felt as though he was looking for something specific.

"What else have you rearranged inside this room?"

"Nothing, I haven't touched a thing."

Turning his head, he leered at her. "Very well then, enjoy

your lunch. The special of the day is a peanut butter and jelly sandwich."

Jack began whistling as he walked from the room, the sound carrying down the hallway. Sara could have sworn it sounded like an old nursery rhyme, but couldn't quite place it. Either way, its frightful tone sent shivers down her spine.

After closing the door, she picked up half of the sandwich, examining it. She took a few bites and then set it back on the plate.

Walking over to the window, she became anxious as she watched the snow fall. A text alert chime interrupted her thoughts. Reaching into her pocket, she took out her phone and swiped the screen.

The message read: **On way, B there 1 hour, Kenny.** She glanced at the time, 11:13 a.m. Her battery was down to nineteen percent. She texted him back: **OK, pls find me if I don't get out.** She let out a breath and tucked her phone back into her pocket.

It's time to up the ante.

Sara went through her pockets to make sure she had everything she needed: *Key fob, check. Cell phone, check. Flashlight, check.* With her duffle bag strapped across her chest, she had her tote bag stuffed inside it, filled with a few important items.

She took one last look around the room, walked over to the door and placed her hand on the doorknob. *What? Oh no, it can't be.* Her bedroom door wouldn't open. Jack had locked her inside the room.

I didn't hear him lock this door. Her pulse raced.

Darting through the bathroom, she unlocked the door that connected to the adjoining bedroom. She hurried to the door. *Please, please, please don't be locked.* Gripping the knob, she quickly turned it. *Yes.*

With one hand inside her pocket, she padded down the hallway, on the prowl for Jack. She tiptoed to his bedroom door and waited for a moment, listening but not hearing a word. She slowly went over to the landing and crouched down, gazing through the wooden balusters. He wasn't anywhere in sight.

She crept down the stairway as quietly as she could, her head darting left to right, on high alert for Jack, but still no sign of him. *I'm almost there. Keep calm. I'm almost there.*

She scurried to the kitchen and over to the door connecting with the garage. Her hands trembled as she slipped the key into the lock, glancing back over her shoulder. She gave it a quick turn and then twisted the knob. Pushing the door open, she stepped into the garage, pocketing the key.

Scanning the wall, she searched for a push button to open the garage door. *Where is the switch?* And then it dawned on her. *I can't believe this. How could I be so stupid? It won't work, the power is out.*

Sheer terror took over as she edged her way over to the garage door. She bent down, grabbing the metal handle at the bottom and tugged at it but it wouldn't budge.

A door slammed from behind, and she quickly spun around. Jack stood in the doorway, glaring at her, his hand hovering over his revolver. She was stricken with fear.

"It is time to deal or be dealt with," he shouted.

Tears streamed down her face as she looked up at the ceiling and said a silent prayer.

"Do not pull the cord."

Blinking through tears, she saw a red rope with a red plastic handle hanging above her. She looked over at Jack, her gaze clashing with his as he took a step forward. Her heart pounded wildly as it raced toward her throat. Reaching into her pocket, she withdrew the flashlight.

"I said, do not pull that cord," he demanded, lunging at her.

She raised her hand to his face, shining the flashlight straight into his left eye. Shrieking, he covered his eyes and stumbled backward.

Sara jumped up, pulled the rope and heard something click. Reaching down for the metal handle, she pulled the garage door up and over her head. She dropped to the ground and rolled under the door. It came crashing down on her duffle bag.

Lying on her side on the snowy ground, she braced her foot against the door and yanked her bag out from underneath it. She scrambled to her feet and started running as fast as she could.

The pristine snow was up to her ankles as she plowed her way through it. With her moccasins sinking into the wet ground, she nearly fell down twice before steadying her pace.

When she reached the end of the driveway, she paused, placing her hands on her knees. Her chest was burning. Her rapid breaths came out in white puffs in the wintry air.

In the distance, she heard the revving of an engine, and for a split second, she was unable to move, frozen with fear. She didn't know which way to go.

She looked to her left, then to her right and took off in a full sprint into the woods. She raced blindly through the trees, weaving around branches, and quickly ducked to the ground behind the tall pines.

The low hum of the engine grew louder, closer. Her heart hammered in her chest as she peered out from the lower branches. She watched as the black Escalade emerged and rolled along the snow-covered road.

Sara remained crouched down until the sound of the engine faded away. Her forest green fleece jacket, flecked with snowflakes had helped her blend in with her surroundings.

Pulling her duffle bag from her shoulder, she set it on the ground and sat on top of it. She let out a long breath, unzipped her jacket pocket and took out her cell phone. A notification read: Low Battery, 10% remaining. With trembling hands, she tapped 'dismiss' and then opened her messages and sent Kenny a text. **'Help. Escaped. He's out here looking for me.'**

Staring at her phone, she shivered, waiting for his reply. Moments later, a little red exclamation point and the words 'Not Delivered' appeared next to her message. Distraught, she sent the message again. It immediately bounced back. It didn't go through. Ten minutes passed.

I can either sit here and freeze to death or take my chances. What was that saying Jack said the day we met? Take the risk or lose the chance.

Standing up, she brushed herself off, picked up her bag and strapped it across her chest. She stepped out from behind the pines and headed back toward the road. The biting cold air blasted all around her as she trekked along, following the Escalade's tire tracks.

The wet snow was seeping through her moccasins, numbing her toes, chilling her to the bone. But she refused to think about how cold she was, or how tired she was. She had to focus on reaching the end of the road. With each step she took, she gained momentum and was ready to run off and hide again if the need arose.

The Escalade was halfway past the lake when a white Jeep Wrangler came barreling down the road. Lowering his window, Jack stuck his hand out, patting the air, motioning for the driver to slow down. The driver of the Jeep rolled his window down and looked over at Jack.

"Where the hell do you think you are going?" Jack said, leering at the dark-haired man. "The speed limit is twenty-five miles per hour, and that is only when the roads are clear."

"Hey, sorry about that," the man replied.

"Obviously you are not from around here," Jack said, eyeballing the Jeep.

"What makes you say that?"

"I have never seen your vehicle around this neck of the woods before."

"Yeah, I'm here to visit a friend. He's not doing so good. I came to pay my respects." The words rolled effortlessly off his tongue.

"You need to know the authorities will be closing this road soon. If the snow does not let up, prepare to be stuck here."

"I won't be long," the man said.

"Well, consider it a warning," Jack's gaze darted everywhere. To the rearview mirror, the right-side mirror, to the left-side mirror, and back again.

"You looking for something?" the man asked.

Jack glanced over at him, hesitating while sizing him up. "Yes, I am looking for my daughter," he said. "We had a little disagreement earlier. She became upset and said she was going for a walk. I came out to find her."

"What does she look like?"

Jack stared out the window stony-eyed as he watched the snow fall onto his windshield. "She is about five-seven, medium build, green eyes, and long strawberry blonde hair. She is wearing a thin, green jacket. She is not dressed properly for the elements."

The dark-haired man paused for a brief moment and then gave a stiff nod. "I'll keep a lookout for anyone fitting that description."

"But how will I know if you see her...if you find her?" Jack's eyes remained blank, devoid of hope.

"If I see her, I'll give her a lift, and take her back home." The man smiled and settled back into his seat.

"Remember to drive carefully. This road allows only one vehicle at a time." Jack raised the windows and drove away.

The Escalade continued along the narrow road, around the bend, to the other side of the lake.

The Jeep picked up speed as it traveled further down the road. Sara soon heard the rumble of an engine as it approached. She stopped dead in her tracks, gave a quick look around and hurried off the road. She raced over to a large tree trunk and stood perfectly straight, hiding behind it.

That doesn't sound like Jack's SUV. The engine...it's different...it's louder.

Sara peeked out from around the tree and saw two small

round headlights coming toward her. Her heart leapt at the sight of the white off-road vehicle. She sprinted over to the side of the road, waving her arms over her head, signaling the driver.

"Help! Stop! Please stop!"

The Jeep came to a sliding halt in front of her. The door swung open, and the dark-haired man came rushing toward her. Her eyes widened as she looked up and saw his familiar face.

"Kenny. Oh, Kenny," she cried out hysterically. "Thank goodness you're here. My texts weren't going through to you. And I didn't know if..." Tears fell from her eyes as he wrapped his arms around her, comforting and warming her. She was shaking like a leaf. "And Jack...he's..."

"Shh, shh, calm down, don't cry," he took a step back to look at her. "You okay? Did he hurt you?"

"I think I escaped just in time," she said, catching her breath.

Kenny guided her to the passenger door, helped her inside the vehicle, and then hopped into the driver's seat. The Jeep's aggressive-looking, deep-tread tires spun around, regaining traction as they headed back down the road.

"You look spent," he said, glancing over at her. He reached for the dash controls and turned up the heat.

"I'm beyond tired, to say the least." Heaving a sigh of relief, Sara leaned her head back on the seat.

"That guy, he's out here looking for you, you know. He stopped me on the road, telling me to slow down."

"How did you know it was Jack?" she asked, rubbing her hands together in front of the vents. "I mean Oliver, his real name is Oliver."

"Well, he...Jack...Oliver...had the strangest look about him. It was as if he were hiding something but looking for it at the same time."

"Hiding something...but looking for something?"

"Yeah, I thought it was really weird. But you know what's even weirder?"

"What?"

"He told me he was out searching for his daughter."

"His daughter?" she repeated, shaking her head confused. "Maybe you misunderstood him."

"No, that's what he said."

"Are you sure?"

"Yeah, when I asked him what she looked like, he described you."

Kenny gazed over at her. She glanced back with a haunted expression.

36

"Something has gone terribly wrong."

"What happened?"

"She is gone."

"What do you mean she's gone?"

"She escaped. She ran away."

"Ran away? What did you do to make her leave?"

"I did not do anything."

"But something had to have happened."

"She lied to me. That is what happened. She stole my key and escaped through the garage door."

"Stole your key? How was she able to steal the key?"

"She shone a flashlight right in my eye."

"Where did she find a flashlight?"

"I do not know but she may have stolen that, too."

"She beat you at your own game."

"Stop it."

"I told you she couldn't be trusted, and I told you she wouldn't last a week. But you wouldn't listen."

"I said stop it."

"You need to forget about it and let her go."

"In this weather? It is snowing like crazy. The roads are becoming treacherous."

"Then don't worry, she will not travel very far."

"I went out looking for her, but could not find her."

"Well, if the snow continues, they will end up closing the road. I'm sure someone will find her, that is, if she doesn't freeze to death."

"Yes, perhaps that man, that man in the Jeep. Perhaps he will find her."

"The man in the Jeep?"

"Yes, he told me if he sees her, he will bring her back."

"Bring her back? Back where?"

"Here."

"Here?"

"Yes, his exact words were, 'If I see her, I will give her a lift, and take her back home.'"

"You do realize something, don't you?"

"What?"

"He pulled a fast one on you."

"No, he did not."

"Think about it. Why on earth would some stranger bring

her back here to the place from which she just escaped? That makes no sense whatsoever."

"But perhaps he is not a stranger."

"Perhaps he's a figment of your imagination."

"Stop."

"Maybe you're hallucinating."

"Stop, I am not hallucinating. I saw him driving a Jeep, a white Jeep."

"Jack, listen to the words you are saying."

"But he said he would take her home."

"Yes, of course he said he would take her home...to her home, to her house...not yours."

"Please stop, I am so confused right now. Please stop yelling." Raising his hands to his head, he pressed his palms against his temples.

"You need to stop doing this."

"Where did I go wrong?"

"I will tell you where. When you convinced yourself that she was your daughter and that she would come back. That's where you went wrong."

"Oh dear, she is not coming back. I was not thinking straight, I was desperate for her to return."

"Let her go, Jack."

"But she could have stayed."

"Let her go. You need to let her go. You need to let them all go."

"But I wanted her to stay with me. I have no one."

"You have me."

"Stop, I do not want to talk anymore." Clenching his fists, he squeezed his eyes shut.

"Jack, listen to me."

"No, I said stop."

"Jack."

"Stop, you are driving me mad," he wailed, holding his hands over his ears.

"But Jack—"

"Oliver!"

37

"Oh no," Sara squealed. "That's him up ahead."

"Quick, get down," Kenny instructed. "You can't let him see you."

Turning on her side, she ducked below the dashboard.

"You need to get in the back seat. There's a blanket back there to hide under. Hurry."

Kenny slowed the vehicle while Sara crawled over the console and into the back seat. Reaching for the blanket, she gave it a quick shake to unfold it. She laid down flat on her back, across the two seats and covered herself.

"Don't stop. Just keep going," her muffled voice pleaded.

Sara remained quiet, listening to the windshield wipers as they swished back and forth.

"What's going on?" she asked.

"Not sure, but there's another car. It looks like he's talking with someone."

Up ahead by the general store, the black Escalade was pulled over on the side of the road. Next to it was a silver Volvo. Both vehicles had their engines running with their hazard lights blinking. Jack was outside his vehicle and standing in front of the Volvo's side window. He appeared to be talking to the woman seated behind the wheel.

As the Jeep drew closer to them, Kenny rolled down his window. He stopped and stuck his arm out, leaning against the door.

"Sorry, man, but I didn't see her," he shouted out to Jack. Raising his hand, he waved goodbye and then rolled the window back up. He gazed in his rearview mirror.

"I feel kinda bad lying to the guy," Kenny said. "He looks so depressed."

Sara quickly turned on her side, bracing herself on the seat and lifted her head. Peering out the window, she stared at Jack in the distance. She thought she would feel anger toward him, after the stress he had caused her the past week. But instead, she was filled with sadness. The look on Jack's face was one of anguish and defeat.

"I think that silver car might have broken down or something. Too bad we couldn't have helped them," Kenny said as he kept on driving.

"I imagine that car is fine," she affirmed, worming her way back to the front not stepping on the seat. "I remember passing that Volvo on this road the day I arrived. Jack waved at the woman driving it."

"Hey, nice booties by the way."

"These moccasins?" Sara glanced down at her feet, rolling her eyes. "They were part of my costume last night."

"Costume?"

"Yes, Jack insisted on having a Halloween party and dressing up in costumes. I had no choice but to play along. I was an Indian and he was a cowboy."

"I'd like to have seen that...the rest of your costume, that is," he looked over at her and winked.

"Yeah, well, I just want to forget it all...forget everything about this absolutely insane week." Fidgeting in the seat, she kept looking over her shoulder and out the back window.

"What are you doing?"

"Making sure he's not following us."

"He's not. You can relax now." Glancing into the side-view mirrors, Kenny double checked to make sure Jack wasn't tailing them. "So are you going to tell me what happened?"

"Yeah, but first I need to figure something out," staring out the window, her eyebrows pinched together. "Why did he say he was looking for his daughter?"

"Beats me," Kenny said, shrugging his shoulders. He gripped the steering wheel tighter and kept his eyes on the road.

When they reached the end of Shady Bend Road, a

white bucket truck was parked at the intersection. Part of the main road was blocked off with orange safety cones. A handful of men clad in fluorescent yellow safety jackets and hard hats were repairing the electrical lines on a downed utility pole.

"What happened here?" Sara asked, rubbernecking at the sight.

"I stopped earlier and asked one of the guys. He told me there was a car accident last night. Somebody ran into the pole and knocked out the power."

"Well that explains the reason the lights went out. I sure hope no one was hurt." She looked away from the scene with a somber expression.

Kenny turned left onto the main road. "Seems like the plows have only been through here once. It might take us a while to drive home."

Home. Sara took a deep breath and exhaled. She had never been so thankful to be going home. She couldn't wait to get back to her apartment, crawl into bed, and catch up on sleep.

Gazing out the window, she watched as the snow continued to fall. Her thoughts drifted back to the day she had arrived at Jack's house. While it wasn't the ideal situation, she had tried to make it work. She just wasn't prepared for the chain of events that had ensued.

"Hey, you okay over there? You got so quiet." Kenny smiled, his perfect white teeth gleaming at her.

"Yeah, sorry, I'm exhausted."

"So, how did you manage to become tangled up with this guy in the first place?"

Sara didn't reply. She just stared out the window lost in thought.

"Okay, so maybe you'd rather not talk about it."

She turned toward him and hesitated. She was afraid of being judged.

"Well, you'll probably think I'm crazy, but I met him online."

"Online?"

"Yeah," she paused, "I met him on a poker site."

"A poker site?"

"You know, a gaming site where you play cards online."

"So you gamble?"

"No, not really, I mean, unless fake money counts as gambling. I used to play at night out of boredom. It was something to do, a sort of distraction from my daily routine."

"Gotcha," he glanced over at her. "But how did it go from playing cards online to ending up at his house?"

"He started chatting with me one night in the game room. There's an option that allows you to chat with other players."

"So he basically stalked you."

"Eww, that sounds so creepy."

"Hey, you never know. There are lots of weirdo's out there. You really need to be careful these days."

"I know, I wasn't thinking straight. I was in a bad place. Here I am, out of work, in need of money to have my car fixed, and he comes along and invites me to a poker tournament at his house. He said I would have a chance at winning twenty-one thousand dollars."

"Sounds kinda fishy."

"Yeah, I can't believe I was so desperate that I fell for it." She took a deep breath. "You know, the more I think about it, I'm not sure if he ever invited any other players."

"What do you mean?"

"He said he had invited six other players, but because of the snowstorm, he had to cancel the tournament. But the way things happened, like everything he did, every move he made, felt plotted."

"Plotted?"

"It was as if I were part of some elaborate game. Like while I was there to participate in a poker game, he was playing some sort of game with me. If that even makes any sense."

"And you thought you were in danger?"

"Yes, well, not at first. In the beginning it was okay. While he seemed a bit eccentric, things were manageable. But as each day passed, things became stranger, and stranger. Then I started to feel trapped. I felt as if I were a prisoner in his house."

"It's a good thing he didn't hurt you."

"Well, he carried a gun. He always had his gun with him and referred to himself in the third person, calling himself a cowboy."

"I'm sorry you had to go through all that. Maybe you should've done some research on him before you accepted the invitation."

"Hey, that reminds me, I need to look something up. Can I borrow your phone for a minute? Mine has a dead battery."

"Sure." Reaching into the pocket of his down vest, he took out his cell phone and handed it to her. "Here you go." Smiling, he concentrated on the road.

"Thank you."

Sara opened the web browser and in the search bar, typed the name Oliver Halvrek. At the top of the page a headline caught her attention. She froze in horror. She felt sick to her stomach when she clicked the link.

38

Double tragedy as mother and daughter drown at Shady Bend Lake

June 15, 1997 - Sylvia Halvrek, 35, and her daughter Samantha Halvrek, 8, died Saturday after drowning in Shady Bend Lake. According to a statement from the county sheriff's office, it is believed the 8-year-old girl wandered away from the backyard and went down to the lake where the family kept their small motorboat tied to the dock. The girl tried to climb aboard the boat but she slipped and fell. She went under the water and did not surface. Sylvia, the child's mother, jumped into the lake and tried to save her daughter. In a statement released by Oliver Halvrek, husband and father of the deceased, neither one could swim. Both bodies were recovered from

the lake at approximately 8:00 p.m. by searchers from the local area.

In shock, tears flowed down Sara's cheeks while she tried to digest the article she had read. With her head hung low, she placed the phone on her lap and wiped away her tears with the back of her hands.

"Sara, what's wrong?" Kenny kept glancing over at her.

"They drowned," she said, forcing the words from her throat.

"Who drowned? What happened?" he asked, concern etching his face.

"His wife and daughter...they both drowned." She gazed out the window, shaking her head in disbelief.

"When? Where?"

Picking up the phone, she tapped at the screen to return to the story. "Sixteen, no wait, seventeen years ago. It said they drowned here...at the lake...behind his house."

"Wow, and he didn't tell you?"

"No, no he didn't."

Her spine tingled as she recalled the dream she had had a few nights earlier. *The lake, the wooden boat...swaying side to side.* Closing her eyes, she tried to block the image of the hand coming out of the water...trying to reach her.

Letting out a breath she turned toward Kenny. "You're not

going to believe this, but a few days ago I had a really weird dream."

"About what?"

"I was in a boat on the lake and a hand came out of the water trying to grab my arm."

"Oh wow, that's freaky. Maybe you have psychic powers," he looked over at her and did a double take.

"No, I don't think so," she said, peering out the window. "But I sensed a dark energy in his house."

"Hmm, what do you mean?"

"I don't know. I felt as if I were being watched the whole time I was there. He kept close tabs on me at all times. But it felt as if someone else was inside the house…as though the walls had ears and eyes. Maybe his house is haunted by their souls."

"You are seriously creeping me out," rolling his shoulders, he flinched.

"I thought I was starting to lose it from a lack of sleep."

"Sleep deprivation can do that to you."

"Do what?" she asked.

"Make you lose your mind, make you go crazy. It can make you have hallucinations…make you see and hear things that aren't really there."

"Are you saying I imagined everything that happened this past week at Jack's house?"

"No, that's not what I'm saying. I'm saying maybe things weren't what they seemed to be. Those deaths had to be rough for him to go through, you know. Losing a spouse and a child at the same time has to be one of the worst types of pain that could be inflicted on someone."

"I know, I can't even imagine…but I wonder why he kept it a secret."

"Things like that can mess with someone's head for a long time. What if he blames himself? Did it mention where he was when it happened?"

"No, the article didn't say."

Staring out the window, she replayed the events of the past week in her mind. "I still don't understand why he would tell you he was out here looking for his daughter."

"Who knows? Maybe you reminded him of his daughter."

"Now you're the one who's creeping me out," she shuddered. "Besides, that doesn't make sense; his daughter was eight when he lost her…and that was seventeen years ago."

"Hmm… well, maybe she had the same coloring as you, similar hair and eye color."

"Maybe."

"And if she were alive today, she would have been twenty-five years old."

"Still doesn't make sense," she said, her voice growing louder. "I'm pushing thirty."

"Ooh, the big 3 0."

"Hey, I just thought of something. My screen name, on the game site. It ends in twenty-five…SaraGirl25."

"Okay, and what was his daughter's name?"

"Samantha."

"Well, there you go," Kenny said matter-of-factly as if he had solved the mystery. "Samantha starts with an 'S' and ends with an 'A.' So does your name."

She looked over at him, pondering his words. "You think he stalked me because of my name and a number?"

"I guess you'll never know."

"You're right. I won't ever know. I won't ever know about a lot of things. I don't even know what's real and what's not anymore. I just spent the last week going out of my mind, thinking he killed some girl and tossed her in the lake."

"What?" Kenny looked over at her, alarmed. "What are you talking about?"

"I thought I saw a body in the lake. I thought it was this girl…Sheila. He told me she vanished into thin air. I mean come on, who just disappears like that?"

Kenny furrowed his brows and kept glancing over at her, trying to keep his attention on the snowy road.

"He has all different kinds of luggage in his garage. They probably belonged to the other girls, the ones who managed to escape his house of games."

"Okay, calm down and don't get yourself all worked up again," Kenny said in a soothing tone trying to quiet her.

"You don't understand all the strange things that happened. I was sick…I passed out. He kept me locked inside the house. I was afraid he would never let me leave."

"Sara, calm down and take a deep breath, you're rambling. You need to pull yourself together." His dark eyes seemed to be judging her.

Shaking her head, her eyes filled with tears, "I'm sorry, you must think I'm crazy. Please understand that I'm not. I just need sleep. Lots and lots of sleep."

"I understand, you had a rough week, but I'm concerned about your mental state. Let's change the subject. Is there anything you do know?"

"Yeah, I do know that I need a job. I'm back to square one again, and under more stress than ever."

"Well, don't get too down on yourself. I might be able to help you."

Sniffling she gazed over at him. "How?"

"The receptionist at Foxdale is going out on maternity leave next week. They've been looking for someone to fill in for her. She'll be out for about two or three months."

"Really?" Sara tilted her head, wiping the corner of her eyes.

"Yeah, I mean, it's not the most exciting job. It's answering phones, greeting visitors, keeping the customer lounge in order. You know, making sure the coffee's made… things like that. It's pretty simple, low key."

"Simple sounds nice right about now."

"Okay, I'll let my boss know and put in a good word for you."

"Thank you. I really appreciate everything. Thank you for

driving all this way in this weather to take me home…and listening to me and all."

"No problem. I like to drive. It helps me clear my head."

"Yeah, me too. How's my car, by the way?"

"It's fine. It's locked up safe in our lot, waiting for you." Kenny caught her gaze and nodded, assuring her everything would be all right.

"I'll be there, first thing Monday morning to pick it up."

"You know, the longer you keep that car, the more it's going to cost to maintain it."

"I know. Years ago I used to have a Jeep, similar to yours. That's how I recognized you on the road. Well, not you, but your Jeep…the two round headlights."

"Oh yeah? Then that's two things we have in common," he winked at her.

Half smiling, she rested her head back on the seat. As she closed her eyes, she could feel the tension leaving her shoulders. They were ten miles from her exit. Sara was almost home.

39

Tuesday, Three Days Later

Kicking off her shoes, Sara flopped down into her beanbag chair in her living room. She had just finished her first day at her new job as a receptionist at Foxdale Audi. Thanks to Kenny pulling a few strings, things were looking up for her.

When she had arrived home on Saturday, she had gone straight to bed to catch up on sleep. She didn't awake until Sunday afternoon. Later that evening, she visited her mother and told her all about her recent adventure.

Monday was jam-packed, giving her no time to think about the events of the past week. That morning the first thing she did was pick up her car from the service lot, thanks to a loan from her mom.

When she arrived at the dealer, Kenny had prearranged an informal interview for her with his boss. They hired her on the spot, and Kenny had taken her out to dinner to celebrate. They shared a Margherita pizza and a bottle of sparkling rosé wine and spent the evening becoming acquainted with each other.

Sara had made a concerted effort not to say a word about Jack. She figured Kenny had heard enough of her ranting and raving on the three-and-a-half-hour drive home in the snowstorm. Sara had only wanted to focus on the present moment and enjoy their dinner and conversation.

After dinner, he had a little surprise for her. He told her that her new job wouldn't be temporary. Through the grapevine, he'd heard that the girl going out on maternity leave was going to quit. Sara became hopeful her new job would work out as she needed the steady income.

Kenny also made her promise him she would never tell his coworkers about the rosé. If his hardcore beer-drinking buddies ever found out he'd been sipping a pink bubbly drink from a wine glass, he'd never hear the end of it.

Sara reached for her spiral notebook lying on the floor next to her. Flipping it open, she unclipped the pen from its cover and stared at a blank page. She bit down on the tip of the pen in her hand, contemplating. While she knew the words she wanted to say, she wasn't sure of the way to say them or a place to begin.

A half-hour later, six crumpled balls of paper surrounded her. *You're making this way harder than it has to be.* She took a deep breath, let it out slowly, and wrote the first words that popped into her mind.

Dear Jack,

I don't know what to say, other than to apologize. Please know I feel horrible for the way I left the other day. Simply put, I became sleep deprived, and my mind started playing tricks on me.

Enclosed you will find your key fob and flashlight. I would imagine by now you've been in the guest room. On top of the nightstand, under the owls, is where you'll find the envelope with the three thousand dollar buy-in money for the game. Thank you once again for the opportunity. Please take care of yourself.

Kindest regards,

Sara

Tearing the page from the notebook, she folded it in half and set it aside. She would send Jack the letter, along with his key fob and flashlight via priority mail the next day.

As thoughts of Jack crept their way into her mind, Sara had to stop them by reminding herself what Kenny had told her over dinner. '*Always move forward, never look back.*' She could hear him speaking the words in his deep, husky voice.

Yet, she still found herself worrying about Jack, concerned for his well-being. After she'd read about the tragic loss of his family, things made more sense. Even though she wished he would have told her, she could understand why he hadn't.

While the past two nights she had held herself back from logging into the poker site, something inside was fighting her. Something was telling her to check on him, to make sure he was okay.

Jack wandered into the study, stepping through the papers lying scattered on the floor. He sat down at his desk, behind his computer, and glanced up at the cuckoo clock as it chimed eight times.

After logging into the Flash Star Poker website, he gazed down at the piece of paper on his desk. Staring at the words, he grinned at the single sentence written in his handwriting.

He first spoke them in his head, and then recited them out loud. "Deal, bet, control, win, find an opponent and play again."

He clicked on room number seven and took a seat at the table. He was alone and sat waiting. He waited for another player, another chance to connect with someone.

It was shortly after 8:00 p.m.

Although Sara wasn't sure if Jack would be in the game room, it was around the time she used to log into the site. She lifted herself out of the beanbag chair and made her way to the bedroom.

She flipped open her laptop and slid into the swivel chair at her desk. As she logged into the Flash Star Poker website, she took a deep breath and exhaled.

She scrolled down the page and entered game room seven. He was there and the only one in the room as if he'd been waiting for her. She clicked on the seat across from him.

Their two avatars sat looking at each other...in a face-off. She made the first move.

SaraGirl25: Hello Jack.

Jack_of_Spades: Sara, my dear, is it you?

SaraGirl25: Yes, how are you doing?

Jack_of_Spades: So nice to see you are safe. I had become quite concerned about you.

SaraGirl25: I didn't know if you'd be here, but I wanted to make sure you were okay.

Jack_of_Spades: Well, I must admit, you played your cards right, unlike the others. You took a chance, and you had an ace up your sleeve.

SaraGirl25: I'll be mailing your keys and flashlight back to you, so be on the lookout for a package.

Jack_of_Spades: You listened and learned the first rule of the game.

SaraGirl25: Let me guess. "Know thy opponent?"

Jack_of_Spades: Yes, that is one of them, but there is another rule which is utmost important.

SaraGirl25: And what would that be?

Jack_of_Spades: Never announce your moves before you make them.

SaraGirl25: What can I say, you taught me well. I learned from the best.

Jack_of_Spades: And so have I, my dear, so have I. We had some fun times together and quite memorable. I will surely miss seeing that lovely face of yours.

SaraGirl25: Please take care of yourself.

Jack_of_Spades: I will, I always do. Oh, Sara, one last thing before you go.

SaraGirl25: Yes? What is it?

Jack_of_Spades: Care to play one more game?

ACKNOWLEDGMENTS

A heartfelt thank you to the following people for helping me bring this book to life. I am beyond grateful for all of you.

To Judy Worman, thank you for editing my manuscript, and for your expertise and guidance throughout the entire process.

To Ana Grigoriu, thank you for a fabulous cover. To see Ana's one-of-a-kind book cover designs, visit her at books-design.com.

To Emily Ives, thank you for allowing me to use your photo of the playing card mask. It's fantastic. To see more of Emily's photography, visit her on Deviant Art @werealilcrooked.

Last but not least, I would like to give special thanks to my best friend and partner in crime. As always, I appreciate your encouragement, patience and unwavering support.

A NOTE FROM BETTINA

Thank you so much for taking the time to read Jack the Shifter.

I would like to know your thoughts about the book and would love to hear from you. If you would like to connect and stay in touch, you can visit me at bettinawolfe.com.

Also, if you have a few moments to spare, I would appreciate if you could leave a review. Reviews are not only helpful for me, but they also help others who may be interested in reading this story.

Once again, thank you for taking time out of your busy day to read Jack the Shifter.

Until the next story,

Bettina

Bettina Wolfe has been creating characters and dreaming up stories for as long as she can remember. When she's not writing, she's reading and has a passion for thrillers. Originally from the East Coast, she now lives in the Southwest.